THE BELL TREE

Another Heaven, Another Earth
The Delikon
The Lost Star
The Rains of Eridan
Return to Earth
This Time of Darkness

THE
BELL TREE

H. M. HOOVER

THE VIKING PRESS
NEW YORK

First Edition
Copyright © 1982 by H. M. Hoover
All rights reserved
First published in 1982 by The Viking Press
625 Madison Avenue, New York, New York 10022
Published simultaneously in Canada by Penguin Books Canada Limited
Printed in U.S.A.
1 2 3 4 5 86 85 84 83 82

Library of Congress Cataloging in Publication Data
Hoover, H. M.   The bell tree.
Summary: On a vacation trip to a distant planet, Jenny,
her father, and their guide tour a mysterious wilderness
which holds ancient relics and menacing creatures.
[1. Science fiction]   I. Title.
PZ7.H7705Be   [Fic]   82-2827
ISBN 0-670-15600-0   AACR2

For Rosie

THE BELL TREE

ONE

A GREAT POTOO WAS BREAKFASTING ON THE RUNWAY, eating up the insects killed there during the night. Some insects were smashed flat and dried. These the bird scratched loose. It fed methodically, deliberately, and as it did so commented on the morning with soft churking noises. Potoos call their name only before a rain.

The potoo is a cozy bird, round and brown and plump. It wears a crown of feathers tilted at an angle and has eyes like deep brown cabochons rimmed with brushed gold, and thick, long lashes. Unlike its distant cousin, the lesser potoo, the great potoo does not fly but walks about its business on sturdy feathered legs. Until men came to Tanin, the potoo had no enemies and even now does not know fear so much as a certain dignified bewilderment.

When the warbler alarm went off, announcing an incoming shuttle, the potoo raised its head. Strange noises were quite common here and did not always mean danger. Still, they were disturbing. While it paused to consider the matter, a great mass hurtled out of the sky and screamed across the runway.

A hot wind hit the potoo and bowled it over the pavement into the bushes. The bird lay stunned, a heap of feathers from which two big orange feet protruded, claws curled tight. Minutes passed before it moved, stood up, flapped off dust with its stubby wings, and peered down at its feet. It lifted one foot, then the other. Both were in working order. It relaxed and fluffed its feathers until all fell into place, then walked back to the runway. New bugs had been freshly killed. The potoo returned to its breakfast.

As the other passengers made their way down the shuttle aisle, the smells of the world outside flooded in. Jenny wrinkled her nose appreciatively, then turned and looked at her father. He had unbuckled his seat belt but seemed in no hurry to get up.

"Let the crowd go first," he said, catching her impatient glance. "That way we can take our time to enjoy first impressions. After all, we're on vacation."

He looked decidedly pale, she thought—a funny green around the mouth. But then he had never cared much for shuttle rides, though she found them exciting. She especially liked the landings when the shuttle came in so fast that gravity pressed the passengers back in their seats and held them there, immobile, until released by the abrupt stop. This ride had been particularly nice, with bouncy air pockets all the way down through the lower atmosphere. Her father had failed to appreciate it.

"Do you feel O.K.?" she asked him.

He gave her a solemn stare and then touched his cheek, arms, knees, and chest. "I feel warm, pliable, and somewhat hairy," he announced in a computer voice.

"Are you sick?"

"My inner ears are at odds with my stomach at the moment," he said, "but simple lack of motion is reviving me."

Jenny translated that to mean that he was space sick but feeling better. Sometimes she wished he would just answer her questions without trying to educate or entertain. At fifteen, she was getting a little old for that, even if he didn't seem to notice. She folded her arms and sat back to wait, the picture of patience, if one ignored the fingers drumming on the seat arm opposite her father.

The shuttle was crowded. There was only one flight a month to Tanin, and it was always fully booked. Engineers, miners, and business people, her father had told her, mostly buyers and importers. She watched them moving past her seat. Almost all of them were men, which seemed odd. Many wore clothing that had seen better days, and some didn't smell good at all. They didn't look as if they could afford the price of the ticket. She leaned over and whispered as much to her father. He sat with his eyes shut, head limp against the seat.

"The shabbier they look, the richer they probably are," he whispered back. "They may be gem buyers, come to buy stones from the miners and prospectors here. Some people won't accept credit in these out-of-the-way places. And then, of course, they'll be carrying gems with them when they leave."

"But why do they dress like that?"

"To avoid attracting attention." His tone suggested his answer was obvious.

"Oh." Since it was their shabbiness that had attracted her attention in the first place, she didn't believe him but didn't argue the point. "Almost everyone's gotten off," she said, hoping that would encourage him to follow. It didn't.

One of the stewards stepped back through the doorway of the cabin and glanced over the empty seats. He frowned at the sight of them and then came over.

"Are you ill, Mr.—uh"—he paused to check his passenger list—"Sadler?"

"He gets sick on shuttles," Jenny explained. "He'll be O.K."

"Oh." The young man glanced from her upturned face

to her father's. "Would you like an anti-traum, sir? I think you need one."

"Yes. . . . Thank you."

"You should have told me sooner, sir." The steward broke a red ampule under the passenger's nose. "We could have saved you discomfort."

"I know. I keep hoping I'll outgrow it. Children are supposed to get motion sickness. Not grown men."

The steward smiled the impersonal smile of those who have dealt too long with the public. "You'd be surprised, sir," he said. "Sit still and let that take effect. There's no need to rush. We don't lift off until tomorrow night." He made a notation on his passenger list and glanced at Jenny. "I'll be at the ramp if you need me, miss. He should feel much better in a minute or two. Here's another in case he needs it later." He handed her a second ampule and walked back down the aisle.

While her father lay silent and pale, eyes shut, she tried not to be impatient. It was boring sitting here. The shuttle was an old one with no windows. She could hear all sorts of interesting noises outside. From below came clunks and thuds and screechings as the freight bay was opened. Men shouted. Something in the bay fell with a crash.

"That was ours. I'm sure of it." Her father sat up. "It's probably irreplaceable here. That's all they ever break—the irreplaceable. Come on, we must go see. They'll make a shambles of our trip before we even start."

From the top of the passenger ramp they saw a uniformed man arguing with several men in white coveralls. Freight containers lay scattered about on the pavement. Freight drones, resembling their lift-truck ancestors only in their hoist mechanisms, were poking around in the bay.

The freight had shifted in flight, and things lay jumbled. The drones, not programmed to cope with chaos, were as often stabbing through or knocking aside containers as they were lifting them correctly onto their flatbeds.

"You have to be *smarter* than the machines!" the uniformed man yelled, and in response one of the coveralled men made a rude gesture with his index finger. "And you can be replaced, Derring!" They couldn't hear Derring's angry reply, which was probably just as well.

"Welcome to Tanin," her father said.

"Are you sure?" said Jenny. "It doesn't look too—"

At that the uniformed man looked up and saw them. "You James Sadler?" He yelled as if they irked him, too.

"Yes."

"What are you doing up there? I had you paged in customs. There's a car waiting for you. You think if you supervise these idiots they'll do better? No chance! I'll have your stuff sent over to the Institute. Go on into the shed there." He pointed.

"Uh . . . thank you."

Her father was never at his best with what he called uncivilized people, Jenny thought as she followed him down the ramp. It wasn't that they intimidated him, although that was part of it, but that they made him shy. He never knew how to communicate with them, as if fearing they might bring him down to their rude level. If they worked for him, he fired them, but he did so with such politeness that some never realized they'd been fired until they received their final check.

"You're sure you know which containers are mine?" he called to the man.

"Don't worry about it. No problem."

"I hate it when people say 'no problem,'" Sadler confided in a whisper. "It's a favorite phrase of incompetents."

At first view the spaceport on Tanin wasn't impressive—nor did it improve with familiarity. It consisted of the field itself, flat and gray and barren, and perhaps six dozen buildings littering an otherwise scenic strip of rocky seacoast.

In human terms Tanin was a fifth-rate planet, remote and undesirable for settlement, known only for its gemstones and rare woods. There was some trade in herbals for use in pharmaceuticals, seashells as curios, and so forth, but that was minor stuff. As they did with a hundred other worlds, humans used Tanin for plunder. Aside from its commercial interest, the planet attracted misfits, people seeking fortunes or escape from personal demons, or people such as James Sadler, who chased the rainbows of learning, always seeking pots of gold others never dreamed existed.

Walking to the customs shed, Jenny sniffed and looked around, trying to acclimate herself in these new surroundings. The town lay below them; beyond it was the sea. That was nice. She liked seas. The sun was rising on the left, making distant water gleam. Beyond the warehouses were hills hazy with mist. The air smelled of lumber and a strange herbal scent too sharp to be pleasing. There was the smell of the shuttle itself, a mixture of hot oil and metal and passenger cabins, and then, as the wind blew, the powerful stink of a malfunctioning sewage conversion tank made her choke and cough.

"That's what you get for sniffing around like a dog," her father said. "Let's go inside."

The customs shed was crowded. None of the passengers had cleared. The luggage containers were just starting to come in, and people seemed ill-tempered. The room was close and noisy.

"They're not automated here," she heard one man complain to another. "They've got *people* handling customs. Can you believe that? There are three hundred of us—"

"Yeah," the other said laconically, and scratched his nose. "If you think this is bad, wait till you see the hotel."

Jenny was fascinated by the man's nose, which had an interesting growth on one side, like a fat pink pea with legs. She was wondering what it was and why he didn't have it removed and what was wrong with the hotel when the p.a. system blared, "Dr. James Sadler, please report to the Ramp A desk. Dr. James Sadler. Please report to the Ramp A desk."

"Where do you suppose Ramp A is?" Sadler stood on tiptoe, peering above the crowd. He looked very out-of-place here, like a blue heron among squabbling gulls, too tall, too thin, too well dressed for the occasion.

"Over there—at the far end." The man with the interesting nose pointed. "It's for VIPs. You can tell because they have a bench there so people can sit down."

"That's very kind. Thank you."

They started across the room, Jenny moving in Sadler's wake as he parted the crowds with a repeated series of "Excuse me. Pardon me. May we get through here, please?" And people grudgingly moved aside until the desk was reached.

Behind the counter was a thin-faced man with dead eyes and an upper lip that tried but didn't quite succeed in covering his teeth. Jenny studied the lip and wondered if his teeth got dry when it was windy.

"I'm James Sadler. This is my daughter. You were paging me?"

Instead of answering, the man behind the counter said, "Let me see your passport." When two passport cards were handed to him, he hesitated, as if his order had been disobeyed and he were trying to figure out how to get even. "She with you?" He flicked a glance at Jenny.

"That's my daughter."

The cards clicked as the man inserted them into a slot in the counter top and then hummed tunelessly to himself, appearing to read a screen Jenny couldn't see. Long seconds passed and she lost interest in him.

At the far end of the counter near the door stood an anxious woman, migraine-neat in gray and pink. She was waiting for a man, Jenny decided, because she searched the face of every man who came up to the desk, and then her mouth would narrow slightly and she'd look at someone else. Jenny didn't remember seeing her on the shuttle, and besides, she looked too unrumpled, not like somebody who'd spent the night strapped into a shuttle seat. Remembering what the freight man had said, Jenny went over to her.

"Excuse me, but are you waiting for James Sadler?"

"Yes! I—" She paused, startled, then made her mouth smile. "You must be—uh—his daughter? I had the impression you were—uh—somewhat more mature—uh—"

"He's over there."

Another uh-er, Jenny thought as she led the way. Before she could say anything to her father, the woman introduced herself as "Nadine Rule, associate director, and so pleased to meet a member of the family. I'm told the last Sadler to come all the way to Tanin was your—uh—grandfather. Now let's see what's causing the holdup with your passports. We can't be rude to the grandson of the Institute's founder! Mr. Dunn, what *is* the problem? Why must we go through this delay each time our guests arrive . . ."

The voice went on and on, punctuated by "uh's" pitched higher than the normal speaking tone. Jenny quit listening and slumped against the counter wall to wait for the order to move out. She felt a little tired now that the excitement of getting here was over. But then, she thought, there were some people who made you tired when you just listened to them, and this woman might be one of those. "Drainers," her mother called them. "They absorb your energy and give back nothing. The true living dead." Her mother was an actress and tended to dramatize things but was, her father said, "a good judge of character. That's why she married me." Her mother was back on Earth, making a picture on a South Pacific island preserve. Island love stories were very popular in the colonies—because of the ocean, her mother said. People who lived in the satellite worlds where water was very costly were fascinated by oceans. They viewed the seas as evidence of wealth.

Her father moved away from the counter, still talking with the Rule woman. Jenny stood up, ready to go anywhere. "Come, Muffin," he called over his shoulder. She blushed, irritated and embarrassed that he would use this childish nickname in front of a total stranger. The woman didn't seem to notice and went right on talking as she led the way outside to a sturdy green box of a car that rode on six ball-shaped wheels.

A seal on the front door identified the car as: "Property of Silas P. Sadler Research Institute, Tanin Outpost." Jenny had grown up seeing that seal in every house and apartment in which she'd ever lived. It seemed odd to see it so far from home, but comforting. The seal pictured a fat brown squirrel standing guard over a cluster of golden acorns. If one looked closely, one could see that the squirrel clutched a tiny pistol in its left paw. A wisp of smoke trailed up from the barrel. The Family Escutcheon, her father called it, and once explained it symbolized frugality, greed, and a sense of humor—the latter quality being necessary to make the first two socially acceptable.

"We can all ride up front." The woman flashed a smile in Jenny's direction.

"I'd rather ride in the back, thank you." Jenny hated to sit in the middle, especially next to strangers.

"Hop in." Sadler slid the rear door open.

"I'll go by way of the town so you can get some impression of the place," their hostess announced. "The Institute's north—uh—by the shore, in—uh—the suburbs, as it were. We're a largely self-contained bio-unit—"

Jenny tuned her out, fascinated by the car's motion as they started off. The tires were so spongy it was like riding on a waterbed. She was going to share this observation with her father, then decided not to, considering his queasy stomach. She sat back to enjoy the ride, looked out the window, and wondered about breakfast.

Warehouses bordered the road at the edge of the landing field. Private aircraft were parked next to them. Some had names that matched the names on the warehouses and were painted in the same colors. It was interesting—but not too. Then, almost at the end of the airfield, she saw something hurry across the road ahead, and she sat up to see better.

"What is that?" She interrupted Dr. Rule's monologue.

The woman glanced over as they passed. "A potoo. They're—uh—very common here. Somewhat of a nuisance—uh—they eat fruit—uh—"

"It looks like a hundred-pound chicken in herringbone

pajamas and a tam," said her father, and laughed to see the potoo stare at them as they passed. "It also doesn't look very bright."

"They aren't," said Nadine Rule.

Jenny thought it looked wonderful. It was real and alive and itself—the first thing she'd seen here that was.

TWO

THE ROAD TURNED RIGHT AND BOUNCED DOWNHILL TO become the main street of the town. Discouraged trees tried to shade the thoroughfare. Most had been barked by traffic, some so recently that the scars still wept. There was no order to the place; buildings stood at any angle, their pastel walls faded and streaked by weather. Flowers grew where they could, tropical and bright. Jenny had never seen so many land cars, all small and battered, parked wherever the drivers felt like leaving them. The few people out at this early hour looked like the town— disreputable but friendly. As the car passed, they waved, and Jenny waved back.

"The Visitors' Center." Nadine Rule pointed to a large pink building. "The hotel occupies most of the space with traders at this end. That's where the miners bring their stones to sell. The Wood Exchange." She nodded at a sprawling yellow structure. "Precious, petrified, and drift-wood are sold there. Down that road, about three miles, is the water plant and reservoir. The recycling plant . . ."

Jenny's attention was distracted by a building with a colorful display screen on its domed roof. On the screen a line of naked women danced and leaped and dived grace-fully into a champagne glass. Bubbles ricocheted to fill the screen and burst to reveal a Pan-like creature, also naked, with a lovely smile. Pan played his pipes and ran away, and the women came dancing back again to dive into the glass in endless gaiety. It was a recreation center, Jenny decided.

"Can we go there?" she asked her father, and he grinned.

"You have to be eighteen," their guide said firmly, and went on. "Down here we have the beach and marina. The bay is an—uh—lovely place. Most of the better people live down here, away from the riffraff of the commercial center." She made a sharp left turn, and the car wallowed on its frame. "On the left is Bio-Dine's research facility. They're developing bacteria capable of making an almost complete protein from the worst sort of organic wastes."

"A true boon to humankind," Sadler said, deadpan.

"Yes—uh—and very profitable. They've been selling patent licenses for their processes. Some of the newest satellite colonies are fed completely by Bio-Dine technology, eliminating the expense of natural food processes—and the wasted space and weight. They'll give us serious competition in time."

"One hates to see space wasted merely for food production," James Sadler agreed, and for a moment the woman paused and looked at him. His face was a mask of innocence. The woman went on talking.

He was beginning to turn green again, Jenny thought, watching him as he listened to Dr. Rule. Jenny could see only half his face, but that half looked sick enough. She reached into her pocket and retrieved the red ampule. Then she reached between the seats and tucked it into his hand. Their eyes met, and he smiled. "We'll be there soon," he promised as he dropped the ampule into his shirt pocket. She hoped so, for his sake. The car wallowed on.

The road wound steadily uphill, past landscaped compounds, fenced and neat. "Research laboratories," their guide told them, "for work too controversial or hazardous for Earth and out of the question in the closed biosystems of the orbiting colonies. Containment problems are solved by the alien planet itself—which is vital where pathogens are concerned. Much of the research necessary to make man adaptive to less than ideal worlds can go on here without restrictions, social pressure, or well-meant but ignorant objections."

"One can create monsters in peace?" said Sadler.

"I—uh—wouldn't quite phrase it that way. It's something that must be done—"

"Are we doing anything like that?" Sadler asked, frowning. "Like Bio-Dine's efforts to reduce us all to phagocytes, able to engulf our own debris?"

"No. It's outlawed by the Institute's charter," the woman said. "Which is a pity—an unrealistic attitude—considering our capabilities and the potential profits."

"I often wonder when honor became unrealistic," Sadler said thoughtfully. "When it became unprofitable?"

The woman glanced over at him; her eyes narrowed and the corner of her mouth twitched before she returned her attention to the road. She didn't talk much after that—for which Jenny was grateful. Her father had a talent for silencing some people with seemingly innocuous remarks. She often wasn't sure if it was what he said or the tone in which he said it, but she puzzled over it sometimes, not sure if it should be learned as a useful skill or understood in order to avoid undue antagonism.

"The trip will be good for you both," her mother had said. "It will give you a chance to get to know each other as people instead of merely father and child. Habit and

/16

routine create buffers, roles one automatically performs, until we no longer see the real character—if we ever did." At the time Jenny had smiled, sure she knew her father as well as it was possible to know anyone, but she was beginning to notice little things. She'd never known, for example, that he suffered from motion sickness, or that away from the familiar, he was stiff with formality.

The road turned into a driveway through an orchard of strange trees with branches elbowing up like candelabra, each branch supporting its own small canopy of leaves and yellow fruit. Each sunlit place was full of birds and butterfly-like creatures that fled from the car, blurs of orange and blue and white. Jenny was so busy watching them she missed the first view of the Institute itself.

"Here we are!" the woman said too brightly, stopping the car beside a rambling brown structure that looked like aged adobe. "We'll have breakfast with Dr. Bower, our director, and afterward you can catch up on your rest. I'll show you your rooms first so you can—uh—freshen up. Your luggage should be arriving soon."

Built around a garden courtyard, the Institute had added wings for laboratories and to house the various research and maintenance personnel. The furnishings were functional but also luxurious. To attract top workers to hardship posts such as Tanin, corporations gave them benefits not given on Earth or in the colonies, and salaries to match. Mechanics lived well here; executive personnel fared even better, with beautiful apartments and private dining rooms and people assigned to see to their comfort.

Jenny nearly fell asleep at breakfast, which surprised her. She never fell asleep at meals. Of course she wasn't sure what time her body thought it was or how long she had been awake. Dr. Bower had one of those sincere voices that lulled. He was trying to tell her father, without coming out and saying so, that he didn't approve much of their vacation plans.

"It's wild country for the most part—wasteland, desert," he said. "There are salt lakes—large inland seas actually. Not much to see at all."

"You've been to most of it?" asked Sadler.

"Myself?" The white-haired man laughed. "Good heavens, no! The idea of that much sky and emptiness terrifies me. It's hard for earthborn people to understand perhaps, but if you're born in the satellite worlds you expect walls around you, to be enclosed and protected. It took me several years to get over my fear of open spaces when I first came here. I still feel very uncomfortable when I can't see a building or some evidence of humankind—a car will do."

"House cats are like that," said Jenny. "They're afraid to go outside, too. The world's so big and they're so small."

Silence fell. The other three looked at her as if they'd forgotten she was there—as they had, since she had been so quiet. Perhaps it wasn't quite the right thing to say, she thought. Dr. Bower had a large head, but he was a small man, as most colonials were, and he may have taken her remark as a personal insult.

"Never having had a cat, I wouldn't know." Bower smiled in her general direction and went on talking to her father. "Had I known that all I had to do to bring you out here to visit was to send you an artifact, I would have done so years ago, Dr. Sadler. To be honest, I was surprised at your reaction. Items like that are quite common here; one tends to put no importance in them. The miners bring them in, sell them for what they can get—if anything. The scroll I sent you was unusually attractive—"

"Do you know where it was found?"

"Only the general area. Miners tend to be evasive about the location of their digs—to discourage intruders and competition. The miner did say, however, that he would like the place better if it wasn't full of so much old junk."

"Where can I find him?"

"He's scheduled to be in town in the next week or so. But a word of caution, Sadler, before you get too enthusiastic. There is every possibility that what appears to be an artifact of some unknown race is often nothing more than the imaginative handicraft of a lonely man filling in a rainy day. Adventurers have been wandering over Tanin since it was discovered a century ago. There are abandoned mining camps and digs in a hundred different places. People with all sorts of talents come here to seek their fortune. The variety of things they can and do create in their spare time is amazing."

"But still I doubt they could weave fabric of a metal never seen before," said Sadler. "Or embroider it with twenty-three other different metallic fibers. None of the metals can be identified. If one ignores the artistic skill and merit of the piece—and both are considerable—the very stuff it's made of is a marvel."

"It was a beautiful piece," Nadine Rule agreed. "I remember seeing it when Simpson sent it off to you. And the little case it was found in—such clever work."

Jenny yawned with her mouth closed. She had heard her father talk about the scroll for months. Not that it wasn't interesting, but how much could you talk about just one thing? What had set him off was a book she'd found in the library stacks in her grandmother's house, a musty old diary written by a man named Arnold Rothman and entitled grandly, "A Journal of My Days on Tanin Written for My Children's Children So That They May Know What This World Was Like Before the Time of Man." It started promisingly:

> *Between the Black Hills and the Baldwin ranges lies the Adan Basin and the desert, a place of rock and scrub and sand. The land here is inhabited by ghosts. There is a lake if one knows how to find it, and caves of wonder hidden in the hills. A great wall passes by the eastern edge of this land and is penetrated by a single passage— a great worm hole of a lava bore aeons old. Only the exiles of Earth come here now, where creatures of inexplicable power and knowledge came before.*

The author went on to relate fantastic episodes of exploration and discovery of lost cities and untold wealth in cut and polished jewels (found conveniently in small cartons which he'd shipped home to Beta One by air freight), and his encounters with ferocious alien animals in which he always triumphed.

Jenny read the book as fantasy but wished that it was true and that she could go there. There were no places left for adventure in her well-ordered world. She told her father of the diary and he read it. His reaction to the stories was enthusiastic and unexpected—he believed them! Or part of them, at least. At first she thought he was simply trying to please her by pretending to share her interests as he had when she was small. But his interest was sincere. He took the diary and a map of Tanin and, using every data source, began to research Arnold Rothman and the man's three trips to Tanin. What had started as her daydream became his—she never quite understood how.

Then the scroll came as a mid-year gift from Tanin and triggered their plans for this trip.

"I believe your daughter is exhausted, Dr. Sadler," Nadine Rule said, and returned Jenny's indignant stare with a superior smile.

"Yes? Perhaps. So am I. You may think it strange that I brought her with me, but I wanted her to see a world like this. To broaden her education. So few people get the chance to travel to a place measurably different from what they know at home."

"She's a lucky girl," Dr. Rule said.

"I'm disappointed," said Dr. Bower. "I thought you wanted Jenny to see basic research firsthand, to see how many years of preliminary effort are necessary to make a planet acceptable for human settlement. Considering her heritage and name, I'm sure she would appreciate it."

"I'm sure she will," her father said, "and of course we have two weeks here now while we orient ourselves and get outfitted for our trip. Exploring the facility should keep her interested. She's quite an active person, somewhat of an introvert, although she makes friends easily. She gets that from her mother." He looked at Jenny speculatively, as if seeing someone else. . . . "She's doing very well in her studies and deserved a break."

It was difficult to sit and listen to people discuss you as if you were an object. People who did that never considered what you truly were. She resented remarks like "she has her father's eyes and the Sadler nose, but her mother's chin and mouth. The bones are good . . ." as if she were a collection of spare parts borrowed from other people and any mind or thoughts she had were incidental or the natural result of genetic influence.

She had been picking little red things out of the remains of her omelette and pushing them into a pile. They tasted like bacon at first bite, but then the flavor altered into something less than wonderful. There was a lull in the conversation, and she looked up to see them all watching her, either fascinated by her search for bacon bits or—having run out of small talk—using her as the excuse for an awkward silence between them.

"Yes, well . . ." she said. "If you'll excuse me, I'm going to bed."

The guest quarters were at the far end of an arcaded garden courtyard enclosed by a clear dome. A fountain burbled amid the greenery. Paths of polished gravel separated flower beds and encircled tubbed white birch, cedar, and seemingly ancient dwarfed willow trees.

She was too distracted now to appreciate the garden but hurried along the arcade to her room and stretched out on the bed. Her father's remarks had depressed her; she wasn't quite sure why. Perhaps because in conversation he had allied himself with strangers against her. Perhaps because she was tired. But she had understood this trip to be a joint adventure and treasure hunt. They had planned it together. Now, by making it sound as if he had grandly decided to give her a treat by bringing her along, she felt betrayed. What she had thought was going to be a vacation he had just categorized as part of her education.

When this trip was over and they returned to Earth, she would begin her seven years of university study. She rather dreaded that. Not the work—she was a good student—but the subject matter: law, economics, and business management. She'd already been allowed the impractical things and had a B.A. degree. She could play Bach on guitar or piano and sketch with an accurate eye. Between tutors and instructors she'd had a good general education, but now it was time, her family agreed, to learn what really mattered. The problem was: what really mattered to them seemed deadly dull to her.

Of course her father had done this, and her grandparents, and they had managed to retain outside interests, but she wasn't sure she could, and sometimes she worried about it. When she thought of those years as a member of Sadler & Company stretching ahead, she sometimes wished she had a special calling, some brilliant talent, that might provide a legitimate escape from duty. But she didn't have one.

She pulled a pillow free of its silken bolster and curled up to consider her current dissatisfaction. She decided she was disappointed because she had looked forward to this trip as an interlude in which, possibly for the last time, she would be free to be herself. Like that potoo by the roadside, she wanted to walk about and gaze at things, just for the fun of it. If she were a potoo, how would she see a car? And while one eye watched the car, what would the other eye see? And did two separate images stimulate two separate sets of thought? She was puzzling over that when sleep overwhelmed her.

THREE

EACH AFTERNOON THE WIND DIED. THE LEAVES WENT limp and still. Insect songs rose with the temperature. It was a local custom to nap during the heat of the day. Not only the Institute but the entire port slept from lunch till after four. Her first few days on Tanin Jenny did so too, not from courtesy but because she was tired. Space lag upset her body's biological clock. Tanin's atmosphere and gravity, close to but subtly different from Earth's, created stress for human cells so differently evolved.

But by the fifth day a half-hour nap was all that she could manage—which left her with a good three hours that were hers alone. She'd never had such a wealth of unorganized time. Life at home was structured, full of lessons, teachers, practice, and friends, who took up lots of time, whether one wanted them to or not.

The first day she woke early she didn't know what to do with herself and, habit being what it is, felt lost and unnecessary. She wandered through the public rooms and then explored the courtyard. The garden was an earthly one, grown by great effort, both as proof of scientific skill and as a tribute to the home world. Roses grew, and dianthus, marigolds and phlox. Red cannas flounced around a fountain and looked quite at home. Not a leaf was chewed. Not a stem was insect bitten. Earth plants had no appeal to Tanin's insects.

In the experimental outdoor plots, the plants from Earth looked weird and were almost unrecognizable. Marigolds three inches tall had shaggy misshapen blooms too large for the stalks. Jenny knelt to study them and wondered if plants knew fear—and if fear of dying here made marigolds produce all the seeds they could in the hope some would survive. She touched the plants as if to comfort them for their plight. Acid seeping from the leaves burned her fingers. When she wiped her hands on her white pants, the liquid left a brownish stain. After that she didn't touch flowers, no matter how much they seemed to need encouragement.

She wandered into the surrounding orchards, hoping to see birds or animals or anything alive and moving. But nothing was. What wildlife the fences didn't close out the afternoon heat discouraged. The trees marched along in symmetrical rows, the soil around them harrowed. Near the base of each tree a white funnel protruded from the ground. Worker drones rolled by, pulling tanks that spouted hoses from their sides. The drones stopped at each tree to pump liquid into the pipe. The stuff smelled rich and vile, but the trees looked healthy and were heavy with strange fruit.

When they'd first arrived, she and her father had been shown the orchards and the fields beyond the orchards where grew native grains and plants that might, with time and tinkering, be domesticated. The Institute's aim here was to develop crops for human consumption. Without them the planet would never prosper as a colony. Until the research was successful, the work was all nonprofit. But if the Sadler agronomists succeeded, as they had on three other natural worlds, then every bit of human food grown on Tanin would pay hybrid royalties to the Sadler Corporation.

She followed one of the drones up the hill, for want of

something better to do, and stepped in front of the machine to see its reaction. It stopped, waited a few seconds, and then began to beep impatiently. When she didn't move, its camera eye swiveled from side to side and, with louder warning beeps, the drone drove around her and continued its work.

There was a fence in the distance, and a gate. Beyond was undeveloped land of tall brown grass and scrubby trees twisted by wind and lack of water.

It was hot coming out of the shade into the sunlight. The way was uphill, and she puffed, noticing for the first time the ten pounds Tanin's gravity added to her weight. After making sure she could open the gate from the outside, she went out and onto the hilltop to see the view from there.

The climb was worth the effort. At the top of the bluff the grassland ended in rocky ledges like giant steps down to the water. Close to the beach the waves had broken the steps into pillars still half submerged at low tide. Brown-and-white birds nested on the pillars. Some birds were gliding on the updraft.

A grove of trees clung to the top of the nearby ledge. In their shade was a stone bench with a low back and arm rests. Jenny went over to inspect it and then sat down. The seat was wide and comfortable and a very nice place to be. She wondered who had built it and how long it had been there. She tugged off her boots, stretched out her legs, leaned back and enjoyed the view.

It seemed so strange to see an empty ocean with no boats, no pleasure domes, no floating habitats—just blue water all the way to the horizon where it faded into blue sky. At home all coasts had been developed. You couldn't

see the water for the buildings—unless you knew someone influential who could get you a permit to visit a Natural Preserve.

From downhill, behind the trees, came a strange sound,
a flat *whee-chuk, whee-chuk-chuk-chuk*. It sounded like a
large bird, feeding as it approached or perhaps marshaling
its young. She sat quietly and waited, hoping to see a
potoo.

To her disappointment, a man appeared. He wore a
hooded gray shirt with floppy sleeves, and wide-legged
pants that bloused over the top of his boots. His hair was
black and cut so short his ears stuck out. He was carrying
a sack and stopped by each tree, where he would take a
handful of something from the sack and scatter it on the
ground. As he progressed from tree to tree, he said,
"Whee-chuk-chuk-chuk." She watched, fascinated.

Intent upon his work, he didn't notice her for minutes.
When he did, he stopped quite still and stared—as she
stared at him. Neither spoke. After a few seconds he returned to his scattering, but now he made no noises. She
couldn't decide whether he was young or old. He wasn't
much taller than she was. She waited until he was close
enough to talk without shouting.

"What are you feeding the trees?"

"Grass seed."

"Why?"

"Grass covers their roots and traps the rain and dew so
they can drink. Of course in time the rain and roots will
crack the stone, slowly, as they have before." He looked
down at the great stone steps. "But that's in long time.
The trees and I are short time. We have to take care of
each other." At that he gave her a tentative smile. He had

dark blue eyes and the longest earlobes she'd ever seen.

"Why were you making that sound? I thought you were a potoo."

"Are you sorry I wasn't?"

"I'm not sure," she admitted.

"Life is full of disappointments," he said mildly. "What you heard was the hunting cry of the horned turtle. Horned turtles eat potoo eggs and baby potoos. Potoos eat grass seed. So if I make a turtle sound it keeps the potoos away so they can't see me spreading seed and the seed has a chance to grow."

"I never heard of a horned turtle."

"You haven't missed much." He shook the last of the seed away and folded the bag into a neat square before coming over to sit on the ground nearby. "How do you like my bench?"

"It's very nice. Did you build it?"

He nodded. "I think about my bench sometimes when I'm in the desert, how when I get home I'm going to sit and look at the water—and then I feel cooler."

"Is that why you care for the trees?"

"People come and go. Trees stay in one place. You can count on them," he said, as if that explained everything.

"Who are you?"

"Jenny—Jenny Sadler."

"Sadler—down there?" He pointed toward the buildings hidden by the slope, and when she nodded, "I shouldn't be talking with you."

"Why not?"

"Because I'm going to work for your father—your father's name is James?"

"Yes, but what difference does that make . . ." Then partial understanding dawned. "Are you the miner who found the artifact? Who was supposed to meet us here?"

"I'm not a miner."

"Whatever. Did you sell that scroll to Dr. Bower?"

"How do you know it's a scroll? It could be a star chart."

"Why do you want to argue?" she asked.

"I'm not arguing. You're being inexact," he complained. "Miners are people who dig for things, who burrow holes in the ground and create ugliness. I never disturb things. I gather what's in plain sight—if people bothered to see. People must stand for something in life, have some essence unique to them. They shouldn't go around being vague and sloppy with all their outlines blurred."

He looked so indignant. She laughed and wasn't quite sure why. "Most of the people I know have their outlines blurred," she said.

"Exactly. You're never sure what they are. They don't know themselves." He gave her an approving smile, and she liked him. He was a little crazy, but then her mother always said everyone worth knowing was a little crazy.

"Why shouldn't you be talking with me?" she asked again.

"Because I'm going to work for your father and you're not supposed to be friendly with your employer."

"Why not?"

"That's the rules."

"Oh." She thought that over and wondered where he'd learned that rule. "I've never been employed."

"Never in your whole life?"

"No. . . ." She checked his face to see if he was making fun of her, but he seemed serious. "My mother's always friendly with her employers. Even when she doesn't like them much."

"Your mother has blurred edges."

"She doesn't! She's very sharp," protested Jenny. "And she wouldn't accuse you of things before she even met you."

"Never?"

"Never! She's a very good judge of character."

"Then she has standards. I apologize." He stood up quickly and looked out to sea, as if he'd heard someone out there calling him. "Good-bye. I'll see your father . . ." His voice faded as he listened to something she could not hear. "Oh, you might want to sit here and watch the moons rise."

"What time do they come up?"

He glanced at his wrist. It was bare. "About five days. They're beautiful. One's blue. . . ."

She watched until the trees hid him from sight, and later heard him whistling down the hill.

That evening at dinner as she was telling her father about the man, Dr. Bower said, "So Eli's back. It always takes him a few days to get around to talking to people after he's been alone in the desert."

"Why?" asked Jenny.

"He doesn't feel at ease with people. I'm surprised he talked to you."

"He's mentally defective," was Dr. Rule's opinion. "He's never said more than five words to me in the four years I've been here. Not that it matters."

Jenny thought that proved the man's good sense.

"He's bright enough," said Dr. Bower. "He's had a rather unfortunate past. His mother was a genetic technician for Bio-Dine, so the story goes, who developed an attachment for a biochemist there. She thought the affair was permanent; the man felt otherwise, and upon learning he was to become a parent, he left Tanin. In a fit of pique she named the baby Gigo and told everyone it was named after the father—garbage in, garbage out. Of course when the boy was older, he changed his name."

"What happened to him?" asked Jenny.

"Uh—nothing." Bower seemed a bit surprised by her question; he'd been talking to her father. "He grew up, as babies do, I suppose."

"His mother died when he was three or four. He grew up with a drone nurse for companionship—and his mother's friends," said Dr. Rule. "There are no children here— uh—normally. Outpost people are not by nature child-oriented. Everyone has a career. One can't really communicate with a child . . . and—uh. He was physically well cared for. But—uh—it's obvious there was psychological damage."

"Shortly after I arrived on Tanin, his mother drowned. Some say it wasn't accidental. Gossip is a popular form of entertainment in our society," Bower added somewhat apologetically.

"I think we should save some of this history for later," James Sadler said. "It sounds a bit—"

"No, I want to know," said Jenny. It was the first interesting conversational topic she'd heard at mealtime here. "What happened to him after his mother died? Who took care of him?"

After a questioning glance at Sadler, who nodded reluctant assent, Nadine Rule said, "He stayed at Bio-Dine for a few years. I'm told he was a very quiet child—very good. He was computer taught, but with little supervision—uh— his education was totally haphazard. He studied whatever he liked and ignored what he didn't, so of course he's unfit for a profession. When there were budget problems and personnel changes at Bio-Dine, he was urged to move to the recreation center to stay with a friend of his mother's. He did odd jobs, things like that, until he was old enough to make himself a house up in the hills. People say he was antisocial before, but he's gotten much worse since he's lived up there."

"Poor fellow," was her father's comment, and Jenny frowned. The person she'd met hadn't seemed pitiful, just different. She stirred what the menu called rice pudding and failed to find a single grain of rice. The stuff had the taste and consistency of a thickish glue with raisins. It was easy to imagine Eli as a little boy. She wondered if he'd seen his mother drown—and what it was—or who—that he'd heard calling him. Rothman's journal said there were ghosts on this world. Goose bumps rose on her arms.

"Jenny?" Her father's voice made her stop stirring her pudding. "Did he say when he'd be here?"

"No. Just that he would. Tomorrow maybe. Did he see her drown?" she asked Dr. Bower.

"What? Uh—no . . . I really don't know."

"And please don't discuss it with the man himself, Jenny," her father warned her. "I'm sure it's something better forgotten. Don't be unintentionally cruel by reminding him."

"Of course I won't," she said, startled that he could think she might. "But nobody else forgot. Why would he?"

FOUR

"WE PUT THE BOOTS IN THE HAMPER AND THE HAMPER in the bay," Sadler chanted as they worked. "Jenny's clothes in Locker B, and Jim's in Locker A. We'll pack the truck together, and then we'll fly her out. We'll go into the desert, and there we'll dance and shout." Hands clasped behind him, he did a neat little dance down the ramp and over to the freight bay, using the grit on the hangar floor to scuff a sand step. His height and innate dignity gave the bit an air of burlesque that made her laugh—as he intended it should. He grinned at her, at ease with himself and the morning.

She was learning she liked working with him. At home he sat in his office all day, talking business to faces on screens, sometimes until late at night, his expression closed and impersonal when she caught a passing glimpse of him through the open door. But when he wanted to, he could be good fun, so long as he was busy and interested.

He'd had the airtruck custom-built and shipped to Tanin for this trip. When they left, it would stay behind as a field truck for the Institute after being stripped of luxuries such as the bath and dressing room modules. The truck had arrived two months before but, per his instructions, had been left parked and locked in the Institute's hangar until he arrived. They had spent the past few mornings getting acquainted with the vehicle and packing their gear into it.

"Where do you want this box that says: 'brushes, waffles, fragile'?" Jenny called. "Is that collecting stuff?"

"Yo!" came the answer from the interior. "In the outer bay next to the toolbox. Easy access stuff. The waffles are for cushioning if we find breakables."

"You think we will?"

"I don't know."

"Yes," said a voice behind her, and she turned to see Eli standing there, smiling. The smile was not for her, however, but for the truck. It seemed to please him very much.

"Dad, Eli's here," she called as Eli rubbed the gleaming finish of the airtruck and then used his gray sleeve to polish off his fingermarks.

"Not a scratch," he said wonderingly. "It's perfect. No one's kicked it or hurt its paint. Such a beautiful machine." He glanced up as James Sadler ducked his head to clear the cabin door and stepped out on the hatch. "A wok," was Eli's greeting as he stared.

"Wok?" asked Sadler.

"Wok." Eli squatted on his haunches to view the underbelly of the airtruck. Sadler gave Jenny a questioning glance.

"What's a wok, Eli?" she asked, since her father would not.

"A night-stalking bird. Like this." He came suddenly erect, transformed into a creature tall and gaunt with hunched neck, wings half-spread, eyes round with hunting as it stepped, deliberately. The beak speared, the eyes rolled dementedly. He swallowed and, as quickly as he'd become a bird, became himself again.

"That's very good!" Jenny applauded the subtle menace he'd mimed. "Can you do other animals?"

"Yes."

"Am I correct in supposing that you've compared me to this bird?" asked Sadler.

"Yes," said Eli.

"It must be very impressive," Sadler said with a laugh, and after a moment's hesitation Eli smiled. "I'm James Sadler. I've been looking forward to meeting you for months."

"Was the scroll *that* valuable?" asked Eli.

"It was that interesting," Sadler said, amused. "As to value, it's a curio at present, unidentified. Valuable for its beauty, certainly—"

"You want me to show you where I found it?"

"If you would, yes. I'd like that very much."

"You'll see woks there. They stalk the shallows at night."

"There's a lake?" Jenny asked, pleased by the idea of water.

"There are lakes." Eli sat down on a carton and clasped his brown hands over his left knee. He wore a gold ring set with a blue stone that flashed in the sunlight. "I won't say which one. I don't want miners there. I don't want you there, either, but that's my punishment for not leaving things where I found them. Or for selling a thing that wasn't mine to sell."

"Whose was it, Eli?" Sadler asked quietly. "Who lived out there?"

Eli shrugged, an oddly boyish movement. "That's like asking what's the real name of a horned turtle. Or a potoo. Or a wok. We don't know what they are, so we call them a funny name. But they aren't what we call them . . . they are themselves. . . ." He looked down at his hands and then unclasped them, letting his leg slide down. "When do you want to go?"

"We have to wait nine more days for medical clearance to leave the port sector," Sadler said.

Eli nodded. "Because you weren't born here. I was. But I don't belong on Tanin any more than you do. You'll see why out there." He paused, frowning. "Or maybe you won't. No one else seems to. Or at least it doesn't matter to them that they don't belong. But they can leave."

"You can't leave Tanin?" Sadler asked. "Some passport problem?"

"No. I have no place to go," Eli said, and changed the subject. "If I take you there you must promise to tell no one where it is. And you must promise to take only what doesn't belong there. You must leave the natural things alone. You can't dig or burn or write your names on rocks or make garbage. I don't want it made ugly."

"We promise," Sadler said. "I know several places I feel that way about. Tell me, are there many things there that *don't belong*? You mentioned our needing the waffle wrap for breakables?"

"Yes," Eli said, although Jenny wasn't sure to which question.

"And you're sure they're not of human origin?" said Sadler.

"You mean did people make them?" asked Eli, and when the other man nodded, "Did humans make the scroll?"

"I doubt it, but—" and Sadler repeated what Dr. Bower had said about miners creating odd things in their spare time.

Eli smiled. "More people should think like Dr. Bower," he said, but didn't explain why.

"Are you going to go with us?" Jenny asked. She liked plans to be definite. "And if you say yes, what's your guide fee?"

"I say yes." Eli got up and went over to peer into the truck's interior. "I'll fly my own truck and meet you there."

"But how will we find you?"

"I'll give your computer instructions before we go. My fee . . ." He paused and frowned. "I don't know. I've never done this before." Sadler named a sum and Eli's frown grew deeper. "So much?"

"That's what I paid a guide on Maxwell's World."

"What did he do with so much money?"

"She put it in the bank."

"Oh." Eli's tone suggested banking was a novel but acceptable idea. "I guess you could."

"You *could* buy more clothes," Jenny suggested rather undiplomatically, "so you wouldn't have to wear the same ones two days in a row."

"They're not the same." The blue eyes regarded her with chagrin. "You weren't listening yesterday. I have ten gray shirts and ten gray pants. I have two black belts and two pairs of black boots and one hundred and forty pairs of black socks. Birds wear the same colors all the time. And animals and flowers. When you see a blue aster you recognize it and say, 'That's a blue aster.' They are consistent. They don't change. When people see me, even from a distance, they say, 'That's Eli.' "

"Rather like a uniform," Sadler murmured politely, "in its psychological effect."

"I'd never wear a uniform," said Eli. "You're not yourself in them."

"At least you don't have to waste time deciding what to put on. You know," said Jenny.

"Exactly!" Eli smiled at her. "I will see you in nine days. At five a.m." And he was gone as quickly as he came.

"Your mother would say Eli had a sense of style," Sadler said as he watched Eli walk up the orchard hill. "Among other things."

"Do you think he's crazy?"

Her father looked at her and gave a sad little shrug. "He'd find life very hard on Earth, marching as he does to his own drum. But here—he may be more sane than most. Are you sorry he'll be with us? We can go by ourselves, you know. I've done enough research so that I can make an educated guess as to where his cave is. I'd rather do that than spoil your trip."

"No." Jenny decided. "I like him. Besides, I have the feeling nobody sees much of Eli even when he's with them."

They passed the nine days in readying the truck. They tried out all the equipment to make sure it worked and that they knew how to use it. Both Jenny and her father prepared a meal in the galley and washed dishes. The sonar stove reduced vegetables to mush in thirty seconds and left them "cooked" but tepid. The water heater was too hot and got turned down. The toilet flushed too vigorously; valves were adjusted.

They slept a night on the fold-down seats that served as beds and found them comfortable. Jenny discovered her father snored. He complained she made her covers rustle like dry paper. They went to the supply depot in town and purchased earplugs, to spare each other future complaints, and a small camp stove.

Once their gear was packed, they flew out along the sea to a high dune area. There they practiced banking, landing, and lift-offs to see how everything rode. One water tank sprang a leak and was repaired. The truck came equipped with a pair of off-road bikes. Utilitarian, they were little more than three fat wheels with power cells, a seat, steering bar, and leg shields. Tested in the deep sand, they performed well and were fun to ride.

Jenny spent her afternoons exploring, particularly the beach, and there, among the cliffs, spent happy hours peering into tide pools that gleamed among the rocks, admiring the brightly colored citizens that swam or floated or walked about in these small worlds. The water was clear and clean, unlike Earth's.

Her favorite tide pool creature looked like a tiny armadillo, orange with white polka dots. It had nine eyes, worn in a spiked tiara, and moved across the bottom on centipedish feet. There was only one to each tide pool. She soon discovered why.

One day she saw a smaller one enter a pool from some crevice in the rocks. No sooner did it start to graze on tiny shells than its counterpart approached, tiara fanning in what Jenny took to be a greeting. Instead, it rudely crawled upon the smaller visitor and hugged tight with feet that stretched like tentacles. What looked like wisps of red smoke drifted out to stain the water. The smaller animal disappeared in the embrace of the attacker. Minutes passed. Fish swam and darted, unconcerned. Sea grass waved in silent currents. When the polka-dotted thing moved away, it left behind a pile of crushed shell that fish darted over to investigate. Jenny watched the armadillo return to its favorite haunt beside a white mushroom-gilled growth.

"How interesting! It's a cannibal." She whispered the observation to herself. She never liked the armadillos after that.

When tide pools palled, she watched the offshore

breakers endlessly mound up and crest and come pouring
to the beach, and she thought long thoughts, as people do
when watching waves.

FIVE

IT WAS THE FIRST TIME SHE'D BEEN UP THIS EARLY SINCE they arrived on Tanin. She didn't like it much. Being up at five was fun if you hadn't been to bed, but to have to waken at this hour was uncivilized. She made faces at her reflection as she brushed her teeth. Her hair stood up in cat's ears. Toothpaste dribbled down her chin. She smiled idiotically and crossed her eyes to get the full effect—and then rebrushed her molars because she couldn't remember if she'd done them.

Her eyes were more green than hazel in the bathroom light, her hair streaked with yellow. "Sun bleached," Nadine Rule called it. "Not good for it at all." Jenny's face was getting brown—not a golden honey color like her mother's skin but more a mass of freckles that overlapped.

The freckles reminded her that once, when she was small, she had taken a green pen and played Connect-the-Dots with her freckles. The game had caught on with her friends—a wonderful elephant had emerged on Mark Bernstein's arm, and Emily Takashima had a star on her nose. They had come home through the park admired by strangers, but their parents had been very upset, especially when the ink wouldn't wash off.

"Jenny? Are you ready?" her father called softly from her bedroom door.

"*Jef abou,*" she answered, and rinsed out the toothpaste.

"What?"

"Almost." She saw him in the mirror, shaved, dressed in dark green, and obviously ready to go.

"I'm going out to the hangar and see if Eli's here. Meet you at breakfast in . . . fifteen minutes." He paused and then gave her a fond smile. "By the way, good morning."

"It's still dark," she complained.

"Have faith, the sun will rise. Even a foreign sun like this. Get dressed now. And pack your vitamins."

"Did you take your motion-sickness pills?"

"Right here." He patted his pocket and disappeared from the mirror.

When she walked into the dining room, he was sitting there with Dr. Bower, drinking coffee and talking.

". . . Eli was waiting for me, leaning against the wall. I didn't see him in the dark. He gave me quite a start. I opened the hatch, let him in. He said about two words to the computer—and that was it."

"And you have no idea where he's taking you?"

"I can only guess."

Jenny pressed the server's button for scrambled eggs plain with buttered toast. She grimaced at the sulfur-yellow patty and brown oblongs that emerged, and dutifully sat down to eat. At least the juice was good.

"Well," Bower said after some reflection, "I guess it's safe enough. If you run into trouble, you can always call for help."

"Yes," Sadler assured him.

"I'm sure you will," Bower said vaguely, his attention now on a file he held out to his guest. "While you're out there, if you come across specimens of either of these grasses, we'll very much appreciate your gathering samples. You'll note here in the pictures the distinctive fox tail of the mature stalk. . . ."

Jenny studied the pictures. The grass had knobby joints and out of every knob two leaves grew. Where the stalk had been broken, a dwarfed floret formed that was quite unlike the seed head. One plant was a muddy green, the other striped green and yellow.

"I realize your trip is recreational," Bower was saying, "but if you did come across them, it might prove profitable as well." He was going to go into detail, but Sadler interrupted.

"We'll keep them in mind," he said, and gave Jenny the file. "If either of us finds them, it will probably be Jenny. She has a sharp eye for detail . . . she's very good at things like that."

"I'm sure she is." Bower agreed with false heartiness.

Jenny gave Dr. Bower her sweetest smile—the one that always made her mother's eyes narrow speculatively.

The morning air was chilly. Ground fog blotted out the town below, gray in the gray light. A large quarter moon hung over the sea; a smaller half moon was setting. Neither one was blue. Birds were up and about in the orchards. Something sang a repetitious trilling song, toadlike in its sweetness. High on the hill two potoos called. Jenny heard them but did not recognize their voices.

Now that she was used to the idea of being up, she rather liked it. From the sounds of things, dawn was the time when local wildlife was active. In the walk to the hangar she saw a number of birds. Small animals scurried about, their shapes indistinct in the half-light.

"Fruit cats," Dr. Bower said, pointing at a fleeing shape. "No matter how we try, we can't totally eliminate the pests. Of course with cultivation their habitats will go. That's something to be thankful for."

Jenny hurried on ahead to where the airtruck waited in

the open hangar bay. In Dr. Bower's mind, she thought, nothing had a right to live but people and the things people could eat. Everything else could be killed off. There was something dead in people like that.

When the hatch first opened, the truck smelled new. She sniffed appreciatively as she entered, stowed away her carry-on case, and slipped into her seat.

". . . appreciate your getting up to see us off," she heard her father say. "We'll keep in touch—after our mystery stop."

"Good. Good. Now don't forget to look for those plants. They could become as important as rice. In their immature phase—"

As a none-too-subtle hint that she wanted to go, Jenny turned on the power. The truck purred to life with a series of smooth noises that, while soft, made conversation difficult for people standing near. It worked: she heard her father's footstep on the ramp and final farewell phrases.

As the hatch closed, she waved to Dr. Bower through the window. He glanced in her direction but did not respond.

"Bower can barely hide his belief that I'm a dilettante," Jim Sadler said as the airtruck began to move slowly out of the bay. "He thinks I'm a dabbler in unproductive enthusiasms unsuited to my heritage and responsibilities."

"What does that mean?"

"He thinks I'm a goof-off."

"I don't like him either," Jenny said.

"Don't give that grass another thought. That's what his field staff's for." He pointed out the window. The sun was coming up, a dull red disk at the far edge of the sea. "Just as I promised," he said, and gave her a grin. "Let's forget about other people and concentrate on exploration and treasure. Deal?"

"Deal," she said. "Is Eli going to meet us when we land?"

"He said he would. Look down." Fog had hidden Institute, town, and bay from view. "We're on our own."

The course Eli had set carried them up to altitudes of more than forty thousand feet, high above the weather, too high for them to see much. They were flying away from the sun, away from morning, back into the darkness that covered most of the big continent. Stars glittered beyond the windows, cold and distant. Seven hundred miles out from port the airtruck made a wide turn from west to south and an hour later veered south southwest.

"Do you know why we're turning like this?" Jenny asked.

"No. Unless Eli thinks it will confuse anyone who might try to follow us."

"Does the computer know?"

"I'll ask it."

But all the computer would tell them was that they would land at 10:33, after a flight of almost five hours.

"Just in time for lunch," said Jenny.

"Are you hungry?"

"Breakfast wasn't very good."

Sadler nodded. "That's what would frighten me most, living in a place like this. I might come to like the food."

"Never," she said. "No one ever gets that desperate."

"Rothman did. Remember? In his journal he tells of the satisfaction he got from freeze-dried. After a time he didn't bother to reconstitute the stuff but ate it like crackers."

Jenny tried to imagine that: if you ate a piece of meat

in its freeze-dried state, when it hit your stomach and absorbed the juices there and swelled up to its full size—"How did he keep his stomach from blowing up? Never drink water?"

"He nibbled a bit at a time."

She made a face at the idea: dehydrated food tasted like dog kibble. What sort of mind would a person have to have to like the stuff?

She turned on the screen to see what the cameras could pick up on the surface below. Dawn was beginning down there now. Between the drifting clouds mountain peaks showed as ridges. Here and there a river flashed silver, then was left behind. The images moved too swiftly and made her eyes ache. She rested them.

"Prepare for touch-down in five minutes fifty-three seconds . . ." The computer's soft but penetrating voice wakened her. ". . . elevation: four thousand sixty-three feet above sea level; atmosphere: benign; temperature: seventy degrees. A wide variety of life forms exists within the area. Exercise caution. Thank you."

"Look, Jenny! It's something out of Rothman's journal!"

If the mountains of Earth's moon could grow trees, they would look like this, Jenny thought as she looked down—old, old rock, canyons sharp and jagged, valleys filled with dark red sand. To the south stood massive rock formations like the stumps of a petrified forest. It was toward the stumps that the airtruck was headed. A lake flashed into view and disappeared again behind the hill, then a chain of lakes. These were obviously not the inland seas on Tanin's maps but small and nameless hollows. As the airtruck came down, she could see across the tops of the big stone stumps. Green bushes grew up there.

"We're going to land beside that lake." Jim Sadler

pointed. "That must be where Eli said the tall birds were. Wok Lake."

And Wok Lake it became.

They stepped out into silence. Even the wind was still. After the drone of a five-hour flight the absence of sounds was disturbing. Jenny yawned and swallowed to make sure bubbles weren't blocking her ears. The lake was lapping silently on a narrow beach of stone and pink sand. In the clear water fish were visible, floating at angles above their shadows on the bottom. Plants grew down there and quivered in some unexplained current. On both sides of the lake, reeds grew in thick profusion.

Paths led to the water. Where no trees grew to block the sun, purple flowers bloomed in thorny clumps among the rocks. Taller plants sported plumes like white bottle brushes tipped with silver claws. The air smelled of flowers and dry rock.

Rock slabs the size of freight containers had broken off the surrounding canyon walls and lay strewn about the area.

"How much do you think that weighs?" Jenny's voice barely broke the silence as she pointed to a slab.

"A couple hundred tons."

She considered that and swallowed again. "You think any will fall while we're here?"

"I hope not."

"We'd be squashed like bugs."

"Flatter." He agreed. "But you will note that trees of some age surround the rocks, so they haven't fallen in recent times. Look at that arch over there—and that grotto." He shielded his eyes to stare up at the towering formations. "Still, it would be interesting to see one of those pieces fall. They must break off near the rim—that nearest one's at least a quarter of a mile away—to see such a mass come tumbling, crashing, slithering down to rest—"

"I wonder where Eli's cave is."

"He'll be along. And as for caves—" He started to point, then dropped his arm. "They could be shadows too."

Jenny shivered for no reason. It wasn't cold, and she hadn't thought of anything that frightened—not consciously at least. There was just a feeling about this place, a sense that they didn't belong here, as if the stone were ancient and watching and hostile toward something so impermanent as humans. How long did it take wind and rain to cut a canyon, to turn rocks to sand?

"In another hour the truck will be in the shade of that wall," her father said. "I wonder if that's why Eli chose this particular spot?"

"Probably," said Jenny, thinking of the shaded bench. She walked down to the water's edge and put her hand in. The lake was icy cold. From this angle she could see far out to where the bottom appeared to drop off into an underwater canyon.

"There are animal tracks all around here," her father called from a spot along the shore. "We scared them away when we landed. Let's get some lunch and see if anything comes out of hiding."

As if their return to the truck were a signal, wind ruffled the lake with ripples and made the trees whisper. From somewhere nearby a bird called, another answered with a roll of clicks. Something living in the lake broke the surface and came down with a splash, then repeated the procedure again and again. All Jenny could see was a deltoid-shaped brown blur that retreated just as it got close enough to be clearly seen in the shallows. She wondered if it was trying to see them.

A weathered snag of a tree suddenly blossomed with a flock of mouse-sized animals with plumed tails clad in purple fuzz. What she had thought were colored leaves had wings and flew. From the bushes emerged a creature that resembled a large black sea urchin with eyes; its means of locomotion was hidden by its spines as it moved down to the water, swam out, and submerged.

Slowly, as her eyes became accustomed to the place and learned to see, it occurred to Jenny that this valley was very much like her tide pools—a small world of its own with its community of creatures.

Eli arrived as they finished their beef stew. They heard a high thin droning that came steadily nearer. A shadow skimmed across the lake, and then a strange aircraft plunked down some fifty yards away. Small, mottled brown, and dumpy, it suggested a hawk moth gone to pot. The hatch opened and Eli stepped out before the dust had settled.

"Where did you find a truck like that?" Jenny called as they went to meet him.

"In the desert," said Eli. "There are wrecks all over. All you have to do is pick up the pieces and fit them all together."

"You built it yourself?"

"Yes."

"Wow!" She was very impressed. "How did you know it would fly?"

"All the pieces flew before. I told them if they didn't want to go back to being lonely junk, they'd better fly again. And they did." He gave the truck's battered flank a fond pat.

"I'd be scared to try that," she said, looking at the truck, wondering if it was safe.

"No, you wouldn't. Not if you grew up here. You learn to improvise." He nodded hello to her father and then turned to survey the lake with a proprietary air. "It's beautiful, isn't it? Not like where people live at all."

"Can I fix you some lunch, Eli?" Sadler asked. "We have a varied menu"—he listed the food available—"or you can have cheese and crackers and fruit."

"I ate, thank you."

"You're sure? It's no trouble."

"I never forget eating—well, usually I don't. Sometimes I forget to eat. But not when I've eaten."

"Yes . . . well . . ." Jim Sadler rubbed his forehead distractedly.

"Do you want to go see the cave now?" Eli asked.

"Right away?"

"While the light's still good. It's easier to see when the sun shines in. Torches make it shadowy."

"Somehow, after coming this far, it seems rather anticlimatic to just rush up and peek in," Sadler said. "After thinking about it so long . . ."

SIX

THEY WALKED. ELI SAID IT WASN'T FAR. "NO SENSE getting out the bikes." It was two miles, all uphill. Both Sadlers were sweating by the time they reached the cave, a fold in a cliff wall where the rock fabric didn't quite meet.

Jenny peered inside and was not impressed. The floor was strewn with boulders, some of them taller than she was. Where the wind hadn't swept clean, sand, deep-layered dust, and animal dung covered the floor. Passageways threaded between the boulders and disappeared at the angle where the roof lowered. The place smelled stale and sweetly musty. "How did you find this cave?" Sadler asked.

"Just lucky," Eli said, and seemed startled by Jenny's laughter. "Well, I was. I nearly walked right on by."

She saw the boy's expression and was sorry she had laughed. Her sense of humor wasn't his. "I believe you," she said, and wiped her forehead dry with her sleeve.

"Now, don't try to pull out things today," Eli warned as he led the way inside. "The dust is deep and powder-fine. When you stir it up, it chokes you. You have to wear a mask to breathe—it's even better if you have a helmet— keeps the dirt out of your ears and eyes."

She went last, not sure she wanted to go in at all. There were boot prints in the sand from Eli's previous trips. Some of the prints were scattered by animal tracks.

"Does anything live in here?" Her voice came back in an echo, "here? here?"

"No." The echo repeated Eli's denial twice over. "Animals come in for shade. Or because they're curious."

Or want to go to the bathroom, she thought.

"Watch out," her father warned as he stepped over another animal's contribution to ecology.

"There's a room where all the good stuff is," Eli called back into the tunnel. "I wanted you to see it now because there's a hole in the roof where the sun comes in about noon. Watch your step. The path slants down and you can slip on pebbles."

"To say nothing of other things," said Sadler.

"Watch your head," warned Eli.

The stone roof lowered until Jenny had to duck and her father assumed a simian walk, which at any other time would have made her laugh but didn't seem funny now. The cave mouth was far behind. The passageway was dark and close. There was dim light ahead somewhere, but it was blocked by Eli and her father, and she could see only intermittent glimpses as they moved. The scrunch of stones echoed. Twice the footing rolled beneath her boots and she averted falling by clutching the grubby rock wall.

When it seemed that she could no longer stand confinement, that she had to get out, they emerged in a tepee-shaped chamber. Somewhere in the cliff above a slab had broken short to form a smoke hole. Through this hole a dusty shaft of sunlight fell and glared off a beige stone wall. Dust motes filled the chamber with a dancing haze. Jenny stepped out into the glare. Her nose tickled, and the resultant sneeze sent dust motes into frenzy.

"Here it is," announced Eli.

But it was hard to tell what "it" was. At first all she

could see was a lumpy floor of boulders and objects half buried in sand and fallen rock. Gradually she could make out what looked like a corroded ball, scattered tubes shaped like baseball bats, matting, and the bones of something with feathers sticking to them. Small animals had left a network of trails over everything. It was definitely not her idea of a treasure cave.

"Interesting," her father said. "It could be a cache or a garbage dump or a tomb." He tried to shift a metallic thing with his toe. The metal didn't budge.

"You can see what I dusted off," Eli said. "The whole floor's full. We're probably standing on things."

"What were you looking for in here?"

"Crystals." Eli gestured into the dimness above them. "A cavity broke up there in the wall and crystals fell and scattered. Some slipped down into holes between things. What are you looking for?"

"The people who wove that scroll."

"They don't live here any more." Eli said. "They didn't belong. They didn't look like any animal here."

"How do you know?" asked Jenny.

"Look at the bones." He dropped to one knee and touched a long gray bone. "There's no animal in this world like that."

"That's a bird. It has black feathers," said Jenny.

"Those aren't feathers. That's fungus. Like the kind that grows on dead trees but different."

"Oh," Jenny said in a small voice.

"Nothing here resembles this?" Sadler knelt beside the bones. "Where's the head?"

"There isn't any."

"Hmmm," was Sadler's comment. "It could be the bones of a native creature, long extinct."

Eli shrugged with the air of someone who knows better and doesn't care what other people might think.

Sadler suppressed a smile. "Have you seen other skeletons like this?"

"A few. One by the far ocean. Two in the desert."

"What did their skulls look like?"

"They didn't have any."

Sadler ran his thumb over the knobby, age-pitted bones that terminated the spine. "Interesting," he said. "Have you ever seen any of these creatures alive?"

Eli didn't answer at once but instead knelt down and reached into a dusty pile of things, carefully, as if spiders might be hidden there. He pulled out a long crystal, clear and glowing, like petrified sherry.

"Ohhh—" breathed Jenny as the stone flashed in the shaft of sunlight. "That's more like it!"

"No. I haven't seen them," Eli said then in response to Sadler's question. He drew the crystal across his sleeve to polish it. "But if they found human bones, would they know the bones were us?" He breathed gently on the crystal and polished it again. "I've found human bones. When I saw them I didn't believe the animal they had been laughed." He half turned and held the crystal out to Jenny. "For you," he said. "Keep it for when you're an old woman and want to remember sunlight on an open world."

"I'll keep it and remember you," she said after thanking him.

"Will you?" The idea seemed to surprise him. "Are you sure?"

"Why wouldn't I?"

"Because you'll live so long. You can't remember everyone."

"I'll remember you." It was a fact, not a promise. She held the stone up to the light and looked at it without truly seeing it, her mind preoccupied by Eli's prophetic promise of long life. Did he know something she didn't know?

"Isn't that crystal valuable, Eli?" her father asked. Eli shrugged, embarrassed. "I don't want to seem ungracious," Sadler continued, "but you might need the income that would bring . . . it looks fairly flawless. Natural gems bring premium prices on Earth."

"If it was flawed it wouldn't be much of a gift, would it?" Eli said shortly. Then he changed the subject. "You asked for fragile things. They're there—that lumpy pile. Keep to my footprints—you'll break things if you step off the path."

Jenny watched her father pick his way across the chamber, kneel again, and with one hand begin to smooth the dust off a domed object. She put the crystal into her shirt pocket, then, fearing it might fall, took it out and zipped it into the big pocket on her waist. The object her father was uncovering glowed like dull blue glass.

"Just look. Don't move it," Eli advised.

"I'll use a jeweler's touch," Sadler promised.

For all his care, when he reached down and gently lifted out the thing, dust exploded as if an air jet had been released from the bottom of the hole. Sadler turned his head away too late. He choked and began to cough, and his coughing made the dust worse.

"Out! Hold your breath!" Eli pushed Jenny toward the passageway as he slid past her en route to help her father. She paused at the entrance; the chamber was filled with a thick sun-yellow fog of dust. She could see her father only as a dark blur half obscured by Eli's form. When the blur of them moved in her direction, she ducked into the low tunnel.

Going in had seemed long; coming out was longer. Halfway through, she had to breathe. Dust instantly sent her into a fit of sneezing, and by the time she got outside, her vision was blurred by tears. She heard rather than saw the other two emerge, their stumbling footsteps rattling the loose stones around the cave mouth. Her father was still coughing, but the sounds were less desperate now. The tight knot in her stomach relaxed a little.

She wiped her hands on her pants and then wiped her eyes, felt in her pockets for a tissue and blew her nose. Her mouth tasted gritty, and it would have been nice to spit. She wiped her mouth and then neatly buried the tissue beneath a rock.

She turned and saw her father sitting on the ground, slapping the dust from his sleeves. His hair and eyebrows were white, as if he had been powdered for an amateur theatrical. About every fourth slap he sneezed. "I should have listened to you," he said to Eli, who sat six feet away, in much the same condition.

"Yes." Eli ruffled his hair, and a small dust cloud drifted up. "You paid for my advice."

She came over to inspect the blue object that had caused all this discomfort. Placed carefully on a flat stone, the piece suggested a child's hat with a six-inch brim or flange that was flattened on one side. The inside was hollow, like a bowl.

"It looks like something out of Ceramics I that didn't quite work."

Her father received her opinion in silence and went on brushing.

"I don't know how we're going to hunt in there—even

with helmets on," she continued. "How can you see what you're doing?"

"You look very closely before you move anything," said Eli. "Then you wait for the dust to settle again."

"What is this thing?" She nodded toward the artifact.

"What your father wanted. Fragile."

"Is it glass?"

"It will break if you drop it. Not into pieces but into tiny grains. I broke two by stepping on them. They dissolved into sand, pale blue sand."

She picked up the blue object. It was feather-light. At the flat side of the flange a deep depression ran from the outer to the inner rim like a pour spout, or . . . On impulse she put it on her head and slid it back until the runnel was against her neck, the brim's flat edge resting on her shoulders. As a hat it was too small. She held it on with both hands and turned to show Eli.

"Be careful, Jenny. Don't drop it."

Her father's voice boomed in her ears like an explosion. She nearly dropped the thing in shock. And then she heard a rhythmic pounding noise and realized it was her heartbeat. An insect noise was amplified to monstrous proportions.

"What is it, Muffin?"

Again the sound boomed through her head. She tried to duck away from the painful vibrations as she lifted the "hat." Her whole body was trembling.

"Are you hurt?" Sadler scrambled to his feet, concerned, reaching out to steady her, but also to save the artifact from falling.

Before she could answer she had to put her hands over her ears to stop the ringing. "It amplifies!" she said when she could talk.

"What? I can't hear you. Are you injured?" Cradling the glass thing against his chest, her father dropped to one knee to look up into her face, as if searching for damage. She took a deep breath and let her arms fall. Her ears still hurt, but bearably now.

"Say something," she begged him.

"What's wrong? What happened to you?"

Relief flooded through her; she wasn't deaf and he wasn't shouting. "It amplifies sounds," she said, and when he frowned, she asked, "Can you hear me? Am I talking in a normal tone?"

"Yes . . . I can hear you fine, but—"

"It's like big ears . . . or something. It makes any noise deafening. Put it on. No—wait till I'm through talking. When you have it slid down so that it touches your shoulders—Eli, when he does that, you whisper something to him. The softest whispers you can manage. O.K.?"

"Yes," agreed Eli.

"If it hurts your ears, move the thing away from your head," she told her father, "because the sound gets worse and worse."

Following her instructions, he put the object into position. It was much too small for him, and he had to hold it against the back of his neck. A strange expression came over his face, and he turned this way and that, apparently listening.

"Fascinating!" he said when he had heard enough.

"I didn't say anything yet," complained Eli.

"I know. Here—try it. We'll keep quiet."

Eli hesitated and then took the device. It looked rather becoming on him, Jenny thought, framing his black hair like a blue halo. But it made his ears stick out more. She shifted her feet and made the rocks chink against each other, Eli winced at the noise.

"I can hear the lake lapping," he whispered, "and a little animal burrowing in the ground down there . . . and insects walking on stones. Their feet click like dancers . . . It's like having the ears of God."

SEVEN

"MAYBE THEY WORE IT LIKE A COLLAR," JENNY SPEC-
ulated as the three walked back to camp. "Maybe they
had skinny necks that fit into that groove and skinny little
shoulders like a snake? And they needed artificial ears?"

Her father shook his head. "It's impossible to guess the
use of things until you know who used them," he said.
"For all we know, the pieces may be drinking cups, or
parts of a computer, or dinner plates."

Jenny considered the kind of face capable of using *that*
as a drinking cup and decided she didn't want to see people like that.

"I'm going to use mine to listen," Eli said. After giving
the dust time to settle, he had hurried back into the
chamber and brought out two more of the strange pieces,
along with one of the cylinders. "I'm going to lie and watch
the stars at night and see if I can hear them burning—
they should make such a roar!"

"You might hurt your ears," Jenny reminded him. "You
don't want to try that where there are people."

"I never go there much anyway," said Eli.

On a ledge high above, a huge carnivore crouched un-
seen and watched them pick their way down a talus slope.
Each time the breeze brought traces of their scent, the
animal hummed low in its throat. They smelled strange
and inedible. Curious, the creature waited until they
reached the tree line, then followed, tumbling down

from ledge to ledge like a dry bush with claws for roots. When the animal saw them next they were splashing in the shallows. She sat down to watch. Often when she chased prey into the lake, frantic swimming would stir something in the depths. A large shadow would rise and make the surface swell; the swimming animal would go under and not come up again. Only small waves would ripple back to shore. But this time nothing happened; the three creatures left the water and walked dripping to a yellow thing that shone like a flower. They stood there, sounding call notes to each other. The carnivore grew bored and padded off to do real hunting.

Since her father had prepared lunch, dinner was Jenny's responsibility. She set about it willingly. Premeasured servings of dry chicken went rattling into a pan. She added water and watched the chips swell into bite-sized chunks. Gas escaping from the tissue made the pieces nudge and bump against each other until the air broke free as silver bubbles that wobbled to the surface and went *plop*. Dried mixed vegetables turned from pastel confetti into bright orange and green and yellow cubelets. Muffins went from dry spitball wads into doughy mushrooms that browned in thirty seconds. Camp cooking was a matter of water and timing; both had to be measured closely to avoid disappointment.

At a folding table he'd set up outside, Jim Sadler tried to learn something about the items from the cave. "They're made of tiny spheroids of a glass-like substance," he called to her. "Each sphere has a liquid center."

Jenny glanced outside and saw he was talking about the blue glass things. "What kind of liquid?"

"I don't know yet, but I think it's oil."

She gave the chicken a stir and added a dash of dry mustard, paprika, pineapple powder, and salt and pepper, then stirred again. "When you know, will that tell us what it was used for?"

"No."

"How about the cylinder?" The chicken began to smell good.

"I bored a hole in it. It's empty. Eli says they usually are."

"Where did he go?"

"Off. Rock hunting." Sadler was more interested in the dials on his equipment than in the whereabouts of Eli.

They saw their first wok while they ate. Dusk was coming on. The lake's surface was reflecting back the orange glare of high sunset clouds. Along the shore, animals were drinking, cautiously, keeping one eye on the airtruck. Other animals lurked among the trees, waiting their turn at the water. A flock of what looked like wingless birds fed along the beach. They darted back and forth across the sand, as synchronized as a school of fish.

"Look," her father whispered. "Down there by the reeds."

A tall gray bird stood perfectly still, its long wings folded in a scissor tail across its back. Its crested head was cocked and listening, and its beak shone like a lance point. When the bird moved to shallow water, the flock of shore birds paused, as if sensing danger, but the other creature paid no attention. Seconds passed; the flock relaxed and went back to feeding.

"What does it hunt?" Jenny whispered. Woks seemed to call for whispers.

"Fish?" her father suggested.

"Why would the little birds get nervous?"

With no warning the wok took flight. Three rapid beats

of its long wings carried it in a glide to a point across the lake.

"What scared it?" Jenny wondered aloud.

"Maybe something in the water—or it doesn't trust the airtrucks."

"Can it see us?"

"Probably. And hear and smell us, too. Pineapple chicken may smell disgusting to a wok. I, personally, found it delicious."

Full of dinner and content, they sat in the hatchway and watched night settle on the world. The sunset glow died. Stars appeared. The only sounds were those of nature, soft and distinct. The cooling air smelled of trees, the lake, and a faint sage-like scent of the pink flowers.

Jenny sat listening to the stillness. "Maybe that's why they wore the blue things?" She voiced the thought as it came. "They landed here and thought they'd gone deaf."

Her father chuckled. "That's possible. Or at least not out of the question. But you're assuming they had separate heads and necks. What if they looked like octopuses—or spiders?"

"So long as they don't want to shake hands," she said, and he laughed again.

A light came on in Eli's truck. The animals went still. Eli stood in the open hatchway, removing things from his pockets and spreading them out on the floor.

"Let's go see what he found," Jenny suggested.

"O.K."

Eli took a can and went down to the lake. By the time they reached the truck, he was seated on the floor, the can of water in front of him, surrounded by an assortment of rocks and pebbles and petrified branches.

"Are you going to wash them?" Jenny asked.

"Dunk them. You can't be sure of some rocks until you see them wet."

From what Jenny could see, he hadn't found much, but she watched as he took what appeared to be no more than a knobby piece of slag, dipped it in the water, and held it dripping to the light. Still studying the rock, he took a small pen-shaped tool from a pocket and used the tool to burr away the green surface of the stone. Without the drilling sound, she would have thought he was painting; his strokes were that delicate. He dipped the stone into the water again and held it out to her.

He had scoured away a thin portion of the stone's crust and exposed a patch of frosty red that glowed as if lit from within. "Watermelon jade," he said.

"How beautiful," Sadler said as Jenny took the stone. "How did you know that was hidden in there?"

"I've found them before. You learn to see."

"I wouldn't have given that stone a second glance," Jenny said. "You're very observant."

He nodded. "In some things. Not all. I'm not good with people."

"People are often a problem," Sadler agreed. "Perhaps it would help to dip them in water?"

"It might," said Eli. "If they didn't expect it. You might get a flash of color you wouldn't see otherwise."

Jenny grinned, thinking of Nadine Rule. Dunked, the woman might come out spitting and swearing, her dusting of phony niceness made transparent and her real self showing through.

"Look at this one." Eli immersed a dull brown chunk and lifted it out. "It's petrified wood. Those are growth rings. That year it rained; that year was dry . . . more than sixty million years ago there were seven dry years . . ."

Jenny watched Eli's face as he spoke. He had what her mother would call "a passion" for stones; they removed him from himself, made his eyes glow and his voice sure and happy. He told them what chemicals were in the stones, what metals gave them color, the pressure, time, and temperatures under which they were formed.

"Where have you studied geology?" Jim Sadler asked him.

"Wherever I could," said Eli. "The computer doesn't know much about this world—just what the satellite cameras tell it. That only skims the surface. I can get more information studying other worlds' geology and comparing them."

"Why don't you tell the computer what you know?" suggested Jenny.

"You have to be important to add to the world data system," Eli said. "Data's only data if you have the right credentials. Otherwise you're laughed at. Besides, I wouldn't know where to begin."

"Have you ever thought of going to Earth and getting a degree?" said Sadler. "Then, if you wanted to, of course, you could come back here and work for us."

"Doing what?"

"What you normally do—but recording what you learn for us."

"And then what?" asked Jenny, and Eli nodded.

"I don't know—adding to the *Sadler's* sum knowledge of Tanin." He smiled at the younger man. "You seem to have a scholar's soul. . . . Think it over. If you want an education, I'll arrange it. No strings attached."

Eli looked at Jenny as if to ask her if what her father said was true. "He means it," she assured him.

"But he doesn't even know me."

"No," she agreed.

"I'll think it over. . . ." He paused to study Sadler's face for a moment, then said, "Thank you. I never had a choice before . . . not like this."

Sadler shrugged. "You'd be doing me a favor. Not to change the subject, but do you know anything about The Wall?"

"That's where people used to go for glory holes."

"Glory holes?"

"Glory holes can be anything. It depends on your dreams. But to miners it means big pockets of especially precious stuff. . . ."

His voice trailed off as he stared at something over their heads. Jenny turned to see. A small blue moon was rising above the cliffs. It looked like Earth without the clouds, and for a moment she was homesick.

"People used to cross The Wall for glory holes." Eli repeated the thought as if in apology for interrupting himself. "They say some people found things there. I've never known anyone who did . . . but they probably wouldn't say anyhow."

"Cut gems? Polished stones?" Sadler asked.

"You heard the stories too?"

"We read them," said Jenny.

"Old accounts," her father said quickly. "Are there ruined cities there?"

"No . . . I've never seen a city. There are things there—like in the cave but different. But anything of value was taken long ago. I don't go there any more. It's too empty. Too sad."

"Sad?"

"The rocks are sad. They mourn at night. Some say it's the wind wailing across The Wall or blowing over hollowed stones—like whistling over a bottle. But the feeling comes from the stones . . . hidden pictures, silent music. The kind that makes you dream. . . ."

Something in the look of him, the sound of his voice, made Jenny shiver. She glanced at her father.

"That impression would seem to verify Rothman's hint of ghosts," he said. "The landscape there apparently makes a definite impression."

"Are you going there?" Eli asked.

"We plan to, yes. The Wall itself is thought to be a freak of nature, a once molten extrusion, thrust up as it met a layer of harder rock—"

"It was *built*," said Eli, not trying to argue but simply stating a fact. "There are openings beneath it."

"Through, it, surely," Sadler suggested.

"Under." Eli leaned past his guests to empty the can. The flung water caught the light with silver that disappeared in a splash. "When you walk beneath that wall, you walk on sand. The rain is washing under. The wind is blowing the sand away. The Wall was built as a fence."

"By whom?"

"Something. Long ago." Eli smiled at him then, a reassuring smile. "People don't like to hear that. It seems to frighten them—to think of who or what had the equipment to build a wall that way—as if it were squeezed from a giant tube of calking with a monstrous tip. But we don't know so many things—and maybe we shouldn't know. They're gone now, whoever or whatever built The Wall. They can't hurt us."

"That boy has been alone too long," Sadler said later,

as he and Jenny walked back to their airtruck. "He's let these empty places prey on his mind. Being on Earth for a while, being with people, would be good for him."

Jenny didn't answer. She was listening to a snuffling noise somewhere across the lake—like a great hunting creature lurking out there in the night, smelling smells and wondering if they were good to eat. It was so dark out here.

They slept that night with the hatch shut tight and the outside air vents closed. Sometime after midnight the hunter left the marshes and set off cross-country, back to its den beyond The Wall.

EIGHT

THE BIKES BOUNCED UP THE TRAIL, THEIR FAT WHEELS
mashing over rocks and fallen branches. Where there was
sand, the tires left furrows, as if giant snails had gone for
an orderly walk.

"We'll ride up to the edge of the talus," Sadler called
back to her, "then walk from there. I'll take the tools. You
bring the collecting bags."

"How about our helmets? They're awkward to carry."

"We'll wear them."

She detoured around a stumpy bush covered with red
flowers and swerved to avoid a sharp-nosed furball. Like
a surprised pedestrian, the creature sat up and stared, then
swore at her in a chittering rage.

Some hundred yards below the cave they stopped and
dismounted. Jenny rubbed her bottom; the bike saddle
was designed for people with more padding than she had.
She put on her fishbowl helmet and felt its collar close and
seal. All outside odors disappeared, replaced by Earth's
air, cool and sterile. She piled the bags together and belted
them on like a makeshift pack, then saw Sadler hoisting
the tool kit to his shoulders.

"Won't you need both hands for balance?" she asked.

"I'm surefooted as a goat."

The trick to walking on talus was timing, moving before
one's weight shifted the stone—but not too quickly; that
caused the stone to tilt and threw one off-balance. Each

step was an adventure. She went up as fast as she could just to get it over with.

Eli was waiting at the cave mouth, a battered helmet and antique breathing unit on the ground beside him. He raised one hand in greeting as she slung the backpack off and leaned against the cliff to rest.

"How did you get here before us?" she asked when she had breath enough to talk.

"Walked."

"Why didn't you wait and ride with us?"

"I didn't want to."

"Why not? My bike would carry us both."

"When you do things with people, life gets complicated. It's easier to walk."

"Oh." She didn't know what else to say to that.

"Besides, we'd have to touch," he said, watching her father struggle up the slope.

"What?"

"If we both rode your bike, we'd have to touch. The seat's too small to sit apart."

What's wrong with that? she wondered, then, thinking she understood his shyness, said, "You don't want to sit that close to a stranger? To a girl?"

"I don't like touching *people*," he said. "People think inside their skins. Animals don't. If you touch an animal, it either likes you and moves closer, or it bites you and runs away. But it doesn't *think* about it."

"Thinking's bad?"

"Where touching is involved."

He paused and half rose to his feet as Sadler slipped sideways and nearly dropped the tools before regaining balance. A dislodged rock went sliding and set off a mini-avalanche of stones that chocked and rattled against one another as they tumbled downhill. "Even shaking hands," Eli continued. "Some men try to crush your fingers just to see if they can—and if you'll let them do it. Others have fingers that smear dampness on you. It's not good touching people. It blurs too many outlines."

"It depends upon the person," she said, feeling tolerant. "Never touch strangers—that's a rule. But I wouldn't mind sharing the bike with you." She paused as her father slipped again, free arm waving wildly.

Eli sprang up and went running down the slope with a sureness she envied. He took the awkward tool kit and cradled it in one arm, grasped the tall man by the hand and towed him up.

"Let's get to work!" her father panted as soon as he stood on safe ground again. He ignored her whispered reminder of being surefooted as a goat.

They spent the morning in the murky gloom of the cave, shifting and sorting through whatever the objects were. To Jenny, it all looked like junk, what she could see of it. Dust coated the helmets so quickly that her left arm soon felt like a windshield wiper from keeping her face-plate clean.

All she found were more rods and capsules, heavy metal rings that might have come from an alien socket wrench, two more glass amplifiers, a piece of metal fabric that looked like scorched burlap, and insects. Lots of insects. They were white and many-legged. Eli called them cave beetles and said they liked dark places. They boiled up out of the dust whenever a nest of them was disturbed. She wasn't afraid of insects, but she didn't like kneeling among them and particularly didn't like to have them running over her hands.

She wanted to quit ten minutes after starting but didn't

say so. If her father was intent on finding more scrolls, the job would be hard enough without her complaining. And there was another point; he often said he'd rather travel alone and be lonely than go with a companion who was a constant griper. So she kept her opinion to herself and went on working.

"This isn't much fun." Sadler decided after several hours had passed. "It might be if I knew what we were doing, but I don't. Since we have a lot of other places to explore, I suggest we call it quits here. How about you, Muffin?"

"I'm ready to go whenever you are," Jenny said diplomatically. That was a favorite line of her mother's; it usually meant: *I hate this.* That Sadler recognized it was clear by the amused little grunt and sniffing sound he made. He had a habit of laughing through his nose. Nose laughs were magnified by helmet mikes.

"We're quitting, Eli," Sadler announced to the figure who appeared in the haze. Eli had been carrying artifacts out to the mouth of the cave. "This is too hard to work without suction equipment."

Outside once more, they brushed themselves off as much as possible and then removed their helmets. Eli carried the items they'd collected to the bikes and packed them in the carryall boxes between the rear wheels. After everything was loaded, he waved up to them, then started walking back to camp.

"Don't you want to ride?" Sadler called. The roof of the stone arch echoed, "ride? ride?" but Eli merely waved again and kept on walking.

"He doesn't like touching people," Jenny explained as they started down the talus.

"The boy's a purist, obviously." He paused to make sure

a step was secure. "I woke up this morning thinking of what he said about why he seldom crosses The Wall and your remark about the aliens landing and thinking they'd gone deaf. What would make Eli use a phrase like 'silent music'?"

"Maybe he's a mystic," suggested Jenny. "You might get that way out here alone."

"Perhaps. But he doesn't strike me as fanciful. He has a very literate mind, little sense of humor, no imagination—but then that's true of most mystics."

Jenny thought of Eli's wok imitation and grinned. He had a sense of humor; it simply differed from her father's.

They were halfway back to camp when Sadler abruptly pulled off the trail, stopped, and dismounted. He appeared to be looking at something down by the lake. Jenny pulled up beside him.

"What is it?" she whispered, thinking he'd seen an interesting animal.

"We have visitors."

From him a statement like that might mean he saw anything from a person to a strange bird sitting on a branch.

"What kind?"

"I can't tell, but there's an aircraft parked between our truck and Eli's."

There was something in his tone that made her apprehensive. A foot shorter than her father, she couldn't see above the trees, so she dismounted and climbed to the top of a boulder. Sun glare off the aircraft was so bright she had to look away. It almost seemed to burn. Yet she could clearly see their truck and Eli's on either side.

"I thought only Eli knew about this place," Sadler said, clearly not pleased.

"Maybe a miner saw us parked here and got curious." She jumped to the ground. "I can't see much in this glare. Let's go meet them."

"I hate people who just drop in without calling first."

They set off again, going slowly to keep the artifacts in the carryall boxes from bouncing out or breaking. Once they reached the tree line, their view was limited, their progress slower still because of roots and fallen branches. Jenny rode intent on the ground ahead, preoccupied with avoiding bumps.

When they were halfway through the woods, the shadow of a cloud passed over, moving swiftly. A gust of cold wind struck her in the face and tugged at her jacket. Branches began to whip and thrash and then went still as unexpectedly as they'd started to blow. From high in the sky came a sharp crack of thunder that echoed and bounced among the surrounding cliffs.

She braked and stopped to wipe dust from her eyes and see what was happening. Ahead, her father was similarly occupied. The sky was full of high drifting clouds, as it had been all morning. None appeared angry. There was no sign of a storm.

"Strange phenomenon," Sadler called to her after scanning the sky. "Maybe our visitors can explain it."

"Or Eli."

"Why haven't we caught up with him?"

"He might not have gone straight back."

Another twenty minutes' ride and the trees had thinned so that the lake sparkled through the leaves. Then she could see their airtruck and Eli's, but no aircraft parked between them. Everything looked exactly as it had when they left camp that morning.

Sadler stopped at the edge of the woods. "Did I imagine that?" he said as Jenny pulled up beside him. "Where did it go? And when?"

"Look." She pointed. "All the tracks are gone. Footprints, bike tracks"—she checked the water's edge—"and the animal tracks."

"Something with a jet wash *was* here."

Branches cracked in the trees behind them, and Eli came running. "Did you see it?" he called as soon as he saw them. "The blue ship? Did you see it?" He was out of breath; his left sleeve was torn.

"Did you?" Jenny asked.

"I heard it leave. That was the thunder. Did you see the people?"

She shook her head and shivered even though she wasn't cold. No craft she'd ever known made a sound like that. "Who are they?"

"No one knows," he said simply. "Security can't pick it up. It's been reported many times, but it never shows up on screen—it's a ghost ship."

"A ghost ship? A local myth?" Sadler shook his head. "Or some pilot getting amusement from creating a myth, a mystery?"

Eli looked at him impassively, then turned and started walking toward his truck, fingering the triangular rip in his sleeve. "I'll have to fix that," he told Jenny as she caught up to ride along beside him. "I saw it once," he added, changing topics in his abrupt way. "It was all shiny with sunlight, and then the shine stopped and it turned pale blue. It looked like a serrated leaf with a stubby stem." He gave Sadler's front wheel an oblique glance. "It's not like one of our trucks at all."

"What else?" asked Jenny, intrigued.

"It's never been seen near the port. Sometimes in

places like this, but usually beyond The Wall. No one's ever seen who flies it." He hesitated as they dismounted by their trucks. "And everyone who sees it gets scared. Everyone I've talked with."

Sadler gave him a long glance and then admitted, "Yes. I felt uneasy. But only because I couldn't imagine who it was, why they were here."

"I think it's because we were in the cave," said Eli. "They don't like people to go some places. Especially where there are bones."

"Who's *they*?" Jenny asked.

"I don't know. I told you, I've never seen who flies it." He opened his truck hatch and disappeared inside.

"I'm not sure, but I suspect we're getting our legs pulled." James Sadler grinned as he opened the freight bay and started to unload his bike. "I think whoever was here just didn't have time to visit, and left. And Eli's giving us a bit of local color as a bonus, perhaps to make up for my disappointment in his cave."

Jenny looked at him; this was the man who less than an hour ago had said Eli had no imagination. "And what if he's telling the truth?" she asked.

Sadler shook his head and went on working. After hesitating, she joined him. He doesn't want to think about ghosts, she decided. Rothman's journal said there were ghosts, especially near The Wall, but he doesn't want to believe that part, just the part about the treasure.

"If you're through with the cave, you don't need me as a guide any more, right?" Busy in the freight bay, neither had seen Eli approach, and both jumped when he spoke.

"I suppose not—" Sadler began.

"So I'll be going." Eli turned and started back toward his truck.

"Do you want your money now?"

"You didn't find anything."

"The agreement was that you show us where you found the scroll. You did that. Hold on and I'll write you a voucher. You can collect from the Institute's payroll office when you get back to port."

"Don't do that," Jenny whispered. "He'll never cash it in."

"No? You may be right."

"Why don't you just give him cash? That's simple and direct."

Eli took the money to avoid the argument Sadler was prepared to give him if he refused payment. "I owe you," were his parting words. He took off, flying west. She watched the small truck disappear over the top of one of the stump formations and wondered if they'd ever meet again. Probably not.

"So much for Eli's secret place," she said when they were airborne later that afternoon. "I'll bet he's sorry he told us about it."

"Why?"

"Because it was special to him and we didn't think much of it. That always spoils things for me."

"Hmmm," her father murmured, preoccupied with flying.

The airtruck banked. The view that had become so familiar disappeared and was replaced by a new landscape. Forested hills ribbed out like swathes of green corduroy decorated by shiny threads of water. As she stared out the window at the land below, she wondered if Earth had ever looked like this. Behind her she could hear her father talking to the air controller and then calling Dr. Bower to assure him that all was well.

"We're going on down to see The Wall, the gate in particular. We should get there by dark. Tomorrow we'll go on into the Black Hills area."

Jenny didn't hear Bower's reply, just his polite questioning tone.

"No. Actually we didn't find much of value," Sadler said, "but it is a scenic place. I don't regret the time we spent there."

Eli was right, Jenny thought, people did talk too much. She could tell from her father's tone of voice that he wasn't really interested in telling Dr. Bower about Wok Lake; he was just being polite, and Dr. Bower was listening for the same reason. People wasted a lot of time being insincere. Or perhaps she was more aware of this because of Eli.

"If subterranean aquifers feed those lakes," her father was saying, "we could irrigate. The climate's quite remarkable. We must make a note to option that sector if settlement becomes feasible."

"You promised Eli!" Jenny said when Sadler had finished speaking to Dr. Bower.

"By the time we're ready to develop this—if ever—Eli may not care and you'll be a rich old woman with vastly more important things to worry about."

"But that doesn't make it right. You promised Eli nothing would change because we came—and now you're saying we'll tap the aquifer and use the water. That will dry up the lakes. The animals will have no place to go. You're planning to make it fields or towns."

"But that's the scheme of things, Muffin—the inevitable result of human development. It always has been. Think what a beautiful town could be built there. Think of that scenery." Jenny didn't answer. "Besides," he said, "I may be wrong and there may not be enough water to make development worthwhile. Don't worry about it."

When I'm a rich old woman, Jenny was thinking, I'll be in charge of Sadler affairs and I won't let it happen. We promised.

Aloud she said, "Dad, don't call me Muffin any more."

He glanced at her, then looked away and smiled to himself, an understanding smile. "I'll try to remember," he said.

NINE

IT WAS SUNSET. FROM THEIR ROOST ON THE LEDGE three potoos watched a shiny yellow thing skim down out of the sky, flash overhead, and circle back to land in the eastern shadow of the wall. Breeze rustled the trees and died away.

A hole appeared in the yellow thing. Two creatures walked out. The smaller one made noises. The larger one exposed its teeth. The potoos checked for gripping claws, saw none, and settled down to sleep.

In the bushes below the potoos' roost a herd of tiny browsers shivered with fear as the creatures approached and then passed by, paying no attention to them. The browsers nestled against one another for reassurance and quickly forgot it happened.

"Try to imagine this gate as it was ninety years ago, when Rothman first saw it," Sadler urged Jenny, "before anyone felt the need to carve his name into the stone. Before the surrounding desert was pockmarked by mines and scarred by tire marks. Imagine standing here alone—no other human for two thousand miles."

Jenny tried, but reality intruded. You could never be sure of a thing until you'd seen it for yourself. Between Rothman's journal and Eli's description, she'd imagined this as a cross between the symmetry of China's Great Wall and a cresting wave of stone, hauntingly noble in ruin. Now that she actually saw it, it looked like a two-hundred-foot-high ridge of rust-colored mud that had so-lidified—an enormous mole burrow.

Unconsciously emulating her father, she put her head back and walked with her chin in the air, hands clasped behind her back to aid in balance as she stared up at the massive formation. Heat waves made watermarks on the sky and blurred the sparkle of an evening star—or maybe it was a planet, to be that bright and close? The air smelled of hot stone and baked clay.

Maybe The Wall had been built as a giant monorail roadbed? Earth used to have things like that before aircars were invented. But it didn't look smooth enough. Maybe it was a dam and this had all been lake? Maybe it was a fence—but to fence out what?

"Do you think Eli's right—that somebody built this?"

"I think that's on a par with people who believe some-one dug the Grand Canyon as a tourist attraction."

"If nobody built it, why is there a tunnel through it? Everybody flies. Everything is desert. Who would want to walk from nowhere to nowhere?"

"The opening is probably a geological freak—an enor-mous gas bubble or a vein of soft stone that wore away."

"Eli said a lot of The Wall is worn away," she reminded him.

"And I'm sure he's right in that respect," Sadler said too easily. "You can see up there, where the shrubs are growing, wind erosion has taken its toll. Geologists study-ing satellite pictures say it appears as if this wedge of the continent had broken off and been glued on again by magma, that this massif is the result of a fracture at least a hundred million years old."

"Did the geologists actually come out here and see it?"

she asked. "Do they know what they're talking about?"

"I don't know, Jenny." There was an edge of irritation in his voice, and he used her real name without hesitation—always a warning sign. "Does it matter? If you'd rather go back to the truck where it's cool, I'll see the tunnel alone."

"I'm getting on your nerves?"

"A bit, yes. I want to feel the atmosphere of the place, to try to understand the effect it has on men—and that's very hard to do when someone is asking endless questions. And, I might add, argumentative questions."

"I'm sorry," she said, and was. She hadn't considered how the place might affect him. There were times when she, too, just wanted to be quiet and look and form her own opinion, without having to be sociable or defend what she thought.

A large insect hurried past, looking like a bark chip with hairy legs. Branches snapped and rustled in the brush along the wall. That meant animals lived in there. Where did they find water here? Beneath The Wall? If it wasn't nearly dark, she thought, she would go exploring and give both of them a chance to be alone. Sweat trickled down her head and made her hair itch.

The entrance to the tunnel sloped down, as if The Wall had sunk. The slope was fine dust, the ground pulverized by animals and old bike traffic. In the fading light the graffiti scratched into the stone looked like tan paint against the rust. "Exit," some wit had carved at the top of the circular opening, and another hand had scratched "Authorized Personnel Only." She wondered how they got up there and why they bothered. Almost every inch of stone around the tunnel mouth was scarred with writing; names, dates, ship's names, cities, obscene words and messages all cried for attention. The latest date was three years old. "The oldest form of vandalism," was her father's comment as he read them. "It all ages into history. Proof that everything passes."

While he went on reading this ancient bulletin board, she walked on down the slope into the tunnel mouth, unsnapped her flashlight from her belt, and examined the place.

It was much cooler inside. The floor was sand, as Eli had said it was, the roof an almost perfect half-circle, rough and darkened as if by fire. Farther in, she smelled something very musky and decided animals came here too to get out of the heat. Just then her light struck mounds of fur, which quickly came alive. She got only a glimpse of beige rumps and long legs galloping toward the opposite exit. By the time she reached that point they were gone.

From the western side of the wall the land fell away in steep slopes, barren and empty and blue in the twilight, bordered by a horizon of black jagged mountains and a massive sand dune. Faint mists floated down there, hovering, twisting, rising on winds she could not feel. The animals had disappeared. There were no trees, no grass. Nothing seemed alive. "The land here is inhabited by ghosts," Rothman had written. She stood here now and believed.

She felt a twinge of illogical resentment at the sound of her father's footsteps, as if an intrusive stranger were approaching—and then her normal self returned. By the time he stood beside her, she'd forgiven him. Minutes passed, neither spoke, and then she heard him discreetly clear his throat. His hand reached up and wiped his eyes, and it occurred to her that he might have been crying but didn't want her to know. Her first impulse was to ask why, and then she hesitated; she didn't know him well enough to ask so personal a question.

"Let's go get some supper," he said, his tone too carefully casual. "I think we'll both feel better after food. It's been a long day."

He took her hand and they walked back together as companions, pretending there was no wall between them. Their flashlights made hills and shadows jerk over the sandy floor.

Long after he fell asleep that night, Jenny lay awake, listening to the wind. It had come in from the east with clouds that quickly blotted out the stars. She could identify some of the sounds: leaves blowing, branches rattling and creaking; the whistling overhead was the satellite antenna. But what was that sudden rush of noise that broke and died away like a wave hitting the shore, and the hollow wail that came from somewhere along The Wall?

A spray of sand slapped against the windows, and the truck shook. The computer's security system, its speaker turned low for the night, murmured, "Landing anchors are stable. There is no cause for alarm. Resume rest." Jenny sat up and peered across the seat backs to see if the noise had wakened him. It hadn't. He slept peacefully, probably snoring softly, she'd have realized if she had been close enough to hear above the wind.

Maybe he was used to places like this, she thought; she really didn't know. For as long as she could remember he had gone away on trips, as her mother went "on location," and she had accepted their absences from *her* life, but never thought to wonder what it meant to them. Were they lonely then? Did they make friends she never met? Did they look forward to coming home, or sometimes regret it?

She stretched out again and pulled up the blanket. What had made him cry? Did that view across the emptiness make him feel alone, too, or lost, or old? Did one feel old at forty-three? When he casually offered Eli a free education, was it a simple act of kindness as she'd thought, or in his mind did it compensate for his plans for Eli's valley? He would gain a man indebted to him for life, perhaps a loyal employee, and Eli might never realize that he had been used. From her father's viewpoint, was that wrong? Or very good business? Eli had no legal claim to that land . . . studying law might be more interesting than she'd supposed. Eli was as vulnerable as his valley, and could as easily be destroyed. And her father was . . . she wasn't sure if she could judge him as a person, or if she should. He was a good father. . . .

TEN

"IT SHOULD BE AROUND HERE SOMEPLACE," SADLER SAID
for the tenth time in as many minutes. The airtruck banked
and lifted at a speed that pressed them back into the seats.
"Damn clouds!"

She didn't say a word. Because he couldn't find the
landing site described in Rothman's journal, he was working himself into a royal snit. People in royal snits were
always angered by anything one said, especially if one was
a family member or close friend.

"You'd think a man with his background would have
been more precise. He was a civil engineer. We've lost
two hours."

"Mmm." She chewed her lower lip and nodded non-
committally.

The airtruck banked and dropped in a sliding turn past
snowy peaks.

Jenny was beginning to feel queasy. They had spent the
last two hours circling and recircling a fifty-square-mile
area. Somewhere in the mountains below supposedly lay
the lost cities Rothman had described, but so far they'd
seen nothing of them.

A great cloud armada was moving over the mountains,
driven by the wind that had kept her awake the night
before. What the clouds didn't obscure they distorted with
deep shadows, making it necessary to fly beneath them if
one wanted a clear view. Many of the clouds engulfed

mountaintops. The computer was kept busy avoiding direct head-on collisions.

After one particularly brisk ascent Jenny pleaded, "Why don't we chose a valley or a plateau and land there? You could get the feel of the place. That might help."

Sadler didn't bother to answer, preoccupied with flying and with the screen before him. Minutes passed. The airtruck rollercoasted down over a valley and up, around the side of a mountain, then down again, through a glaring white cloud and out. Rain flecked the windows.

"If we don't land soon, I'm going to throw up," she announced quietly. She didn't want to get dramatic, but her situation was desperate.

"Take a whiff of anti-traum," came the distracted answer. His expression said her complaint was an inconvenience.

"I did. It didn't help. Why aren't you sick?"

"Never when I'm in control. Why are you? You never get sick."

"I am now."

Something in her voice made him finally look at her. "You *are*, aren't you? Hang on. We'll get you on firm ground in a minute."

To keep her mind off her problem, she concentrated on the blue light digits in the clock. Three hundred very long seconds ticked off before she felt the gentle shock of landing, ten more before the hatch opened. Cool air came in and with it a wonderful smell. She took a deep breath, leaned back, and closed her eyes.

Sadler reached over, released her seat belt, and put the seat into reclining position. "I'll get a cold compress." When he'd done all he could without becoming a bother, he went outside to give her time to recover. She heard tall grass brush against his legs as he walked away. A bird sang. The wind blew in the open door. The waves of sickness went away.

They had landed on a mountain meadow so high that clouds drifted past below. When, ten minutes later, Jenny stood looking down at them, she felt a frightening urge to run and jump into their softness, sure they would buoy her up.

She looked away, out across the mountains. Sadler, thinking she had heard something in the distance, followed her gaze with his binoculars. "It's an aircraft." She glanced at him, not knowing what he was talking about. "The thing you're watching—it's an aircraft."

Without the binoculars it looked like a speck, a distant bird or insect. When she blinked she lost sight of it and found it again only as its shadow fled over a pale bluff. That moth shape was unmistakable. "It's Eli!"

"I think he's coming here!" Sadler said, surprised. The speck banked in a lazy half circle and grew larger, disappeared in a giant cloud—which Jenny found alarming— re-emerged, trailing wisps, only to be swallowed up again. From her perspective the clouds looked substantial, while the tiny flying machine seemed almost unreal until it grew close enough to circle for a landing.

"You can see that yellow for miles, you know," Eli announced as he got out. "Are you in some sort of trouble?"

"I got airsick," Jenny said. "Besides, we're lost."

"We're not *lost*," Sadler said. "We just haven't found where we wanted to go, as yet." Not all the snit had disappeared.

Eli plucked a stalk of the sweet grass, rolled it between his palms to bruise it, then wiped his hands on his pants.

"I saw you fly over four times. You went a different direction each time. None of them was the right way."

"And you know the right way?"

"I know where you want to go."

"What are you doing in these mountains?" Sadler asked. "I got the impression you didn't like it here."

"I don't," the boy said, "but you hired me as a guide, and you didn't want what I guided you to, so I owe you."

"That's not necessary—"

"Yes, it is," said Jenny, who was glad to see him again. "You said yourself we were wasting time. And even if Eli's wrong, he can't be any wronger than we've been. Right?"

"I suppose not."

They let Eli get a headstart since his craft was slower. He led them, not southwest as Sadler had decided, but east, back into the foothills less than twenty miles from where The Wall sloped down and disappeared into the sea.

"This can't be right," Sadler kept repeating. "Miners would have been all over this area. . . . He's slowing down to land."

Below them a river snaked through a wooded pocket between low hills, backed by eroded cliffs honeycombed with holes and flanked by pinnacles and hoodoos of beige and pink sandstone. A body of dark water in the shape of a half moon curved around the high end of the valley and carved its way beneath a cliff so that half its surface lay in constant shade. To the east the land sloped miles to the floor of the desert that stretched all the way to The Wall.

A herd of animals, frightened by Eli's truck, ran across the open, a rug of bobbing brown backs fringed by puffs of dust. Others fled or stood watching the yellow truck hover above the treetops. The animals looked bewildered,

Jenny thought, as if they couldn't understand what they were seeing.

Tall trees like ancient jade plants bordered the open side of the lake, their brown roots gnarled down into the rock and sand beneath them, anchoring trunks that were massive and twisted. Their waxy leaves were the size of dinner plates and almost translucent green.

"How weird," was Jenny's whispered opinion as the hatch slid open and framed a tree. Wind made the sunshine cold, but the lake didn't ripple.

"One can understand how a place like this would affect the imagination," Sadler said. "It looks unreal, like something a mad landscape architect designed."

"I think one did," Jenny said, thinking of the orchard rows. "Those trees are spaced too evenly to be wild. Those were planted."

He glanced from her face to the trees and back again, then nodded and smiled for the first time that day. "I think you may be right! They look like ornamentals."

He hurried over to inspect the nearest tree, and she followed but kept looking back, wondering why Eli didn't join them. She saw him emerge with a toolbox and crawl under his truck. After a minute or so the blue arc of a welding torch lit up the underbelly.

"Jenny? Look at this—I don't think it's real." The awe in Sadler's voice made her turn. He was squatting down beside the tree, running his hand over the spiral twist of its trunk. "I think it's made of metal." While he detached a series of tools from his belt and prepared to do some tests, Jenny simply picked up a rock and hammered on the nearest root, which rang.

"You're right," she said and, taking casual aim, tossed

her rock at the leaves above. The rock hit a leaf and shattered into fragments that fell into the water. The leaf rang a deep resonant *bong.* She laughed with pure delight. "Did you hear that? It's a bell tree! Did you hear?"

"I heard." He shook his head as if to clear water from his ears. "When you hit the root, I leaned closer to monitor the vibrations, and then you rang that chime . . . I hate it when you do scientific testing." He paused. "Actually that was quick thinking—very smart. Why didn't I think of that?"

"You're overeducated. When you learn too much you forget the easy stuff."

"That's true," he agreed with no attempt at humor. "Now, if you'll leave me alone for a few minutes, maybe I can learn particulars."

"What if I go find a pole long enough to hit the leaves?" she suggested. "So we can play them?"

"Later, perhaps?"

She grinned and agreed. "O.K. I'll go talk to Eli."

All she could see of Eli was one boot protruding from beneath his truck, but she could hear him muttering to himself as he worked.

"Eli?" she called. The muttering stopped. "Eli?"

"Yes?"

"Did you know the trees around the lake aren't real?" The only response she got was the clicking whir of a socket wrench. "Eli?"

"The lake isn't real either."

She considered that and decided to ignore it for the moment. "You knew about the trees?"

"Yes. I was here once when it rained. Stones just don't get the right tone." The wrench chattered again.

She stood there beside his foot, feeling rather deflated because he knew more about her discovery than she did. Then she remembered. "What about the lake?"

"It's cut out of the rock and laser-glazed." He interrupted himself to hammer something. "They piped in water from the river. There are fountains down in there. And outlet vents."

"How do you know?"

"I swam down to look."

"How come you didn't tell us all this?"

"You didn't ask me." He hammered again. "You just said you wanted to see old cities."

"This doesn't look like a city. Where is it?"

The boot beside her was joined by its mate, and after a moment he pushed himself out from under the truck. He was wearing a bug-eyed welding hood to protect his face.

"There were buildings all around us," he said. "We're standing where one stood. There." He pointed toward the hill of trees. "There's a horned turtle's burrow big enough to crawl into. It has a blue shiny floor in its sleeping chamber. Where the tallest trees are—those are real—" He reached up and pulled his hood off, and Jenny saw the goggles had left a ringed imprint around his eyes. "You can see the sections of old walls."

"Why don't the miners come here?"

"Nothing shows on aerial maps that would make it worth the bother. Once you land, you have to walk because of the river. Miners don't like to walk. Rocks are too heavy to carry."

"But it's a pretty place."

"There are lots of pretty places," Eli said. "Besides, miners don't care about pretty."

The scrunch of footsteps made them glance up to see

Sadler approaching. "It's fascinating! Absolutely fascinating! I took a core sample with the laser drill—that tree is made of the same stuff as that scroll you found. Only here they've used metal to simulate cellulose."

Eli and Jenny looked at him, not sure how to respond. "What does that mean?" asked Jenny. "Other than it was made by the same people."

Sadler frowned and opened his mouth to speak, then closed it again. "I don't know," he admitted, and his enthusiasm faded for lack of someone to share it with.

ELEVEN

IN THE DARKNESS OF HER DEN THE GHEMA CAME AWAKE
and raised her head from her massive paws. There were
noises. Not the sound of falling stone, or frantic wingbeats
of lost birds, or rain on trees and waterhole—some strange
animal was out there. She sniffed the air and coughed to
check its taste. The wind was coming from rear passages
and blurred the scent. The den smelled as it had for forty
years—a satisfying sweetness of rotting pelts and bones
and old blood, stone and lichen, musky insects, and the
small furry scavengers who made their living from her
leavings. Because they kept her quarters neat, she ate
them only in the rainy season, when she was bored at
being den bound.

The noise came again, clearly now. Closer. Footfalls on
the stone and sand around the waterhole. But what sort
of creature walked on six paws, with three separate ca-
dences? Or was it six hooves? She couldn't be sure. The
footfalls stopped, and the animal or animals vocalized. A
bird voice, a song of three distinct tones, followed by two
deeper songs. But they didn't walk like birds. They were
too sure, too confident. They walked like carnivores. Like
herself. The ghema growled softly, twitched her tail, got
up, and padded to the arched doorway. Although she
weighed twelve hundred pounds, the clicking of her claws
on the stone was the only sound she made in walking.

She was halfway down the corridor when she recognized the scent. They had followed her, the strange creatures from the yellow thing.

The temperature dropped noticeably beneath the overhanging cliff. The water made dancing reflections on the curved ceiling. Jenny had been walking backward most of the way, the better to watch the curious animals who followed them. Once over their initial fright of the airtrucks, the animals had returned. At first shyly, then with increasing boldness, they had watched them eat their lunch. They had sniffed the trucks, crawled beneath them if they could, crowded about the open hatch and stared inside, and finally several had walked up the ramp and tried to enter. Eli said the animals were all like this where humans seldom came. Jenny was delighted, her father less so. He reacted to the animals as he did to people with bad manners; he found them offensive but didn't know how to deal with them without appearing to be equally rude.

As the mixed herd neared the overhang, their pace slowed. Several black-and-white grazers stopped and bleated nervously, then fled. A gray-and-brown browser with elegant long legs turned away and went to feeding on a branch, then suddenly galloped out of sight among the trees. At the sound of hoofbeats the other animals looked up, then seemed to recall that they had business elsewhere.

"The animals don't like it in the shade," Jenny informed the other two. "They're running away."

"Good," said Sadler without looking back.

"They don't like to feel closed in," Eli called. He led the way. They were en route to the cliff walls to the right of the overhang, a place where he said some of the niches looked more like rooms than wind-eroded caves. The berm of the lake afforded the easiest path.

The farther she walked under this stone canopy, the more Jenny understood the animals' reaction. Not only was it cold and dim, but it was oppressive. She peered up at the ceiling where light shifted with each breeze on the water's surface, followed the ceiling's curve over to the rear wall where it became a mass of blackness. She could see a wide shelf on the other side of the water and what looked like a ledge or ramp leading up the cliff.

"Is that a ramp over there, beneath the dome?" she called to Eli.

"I don't know," he answered when the echo of her voice died away, so he could be heard. "I never went back there."

"Don't dawdle, Jenny," Sadler urged, turning to see her standing some fifteen yards behind, staring off into the darkness. "That's one thing you have to learn to accept on trips; you have time for only so much. You can't see everything. You have to opt for what's worthwhile."

"Yes, sir," she said obediently, and ran to catch up. But she'd already decided that when they reached the end of the pool she was going to make a quick detour and see that ledge. Probably it just dead-ended in the cliff, but it was worth a look. She put her hand on her torch to make sure it was ready.

As they came out into the open, Eli turned right to lead them downhill, past a forest of hoodoos interspersed with trees. Jenny hesitated and then said, "I'll be right back."

"Jenny!"

"Be right back!"

The rear ledge was wider than it looked from across the lake and was covered with sand dimpled by animal tracks. Branches lay scattered, blown in by storms, and rocks had tumbled from the wall and grown moss. She used the light to pick her way over the litter. The base of the ramp was buried in sand, but its surface and outer edge looked too uniform to be a natural formation, and the angle of assent too engineered. Wind had blown the slope clean.

"Jenny?" Her father sounded irked.

"Come look at this," she called as she started up the ramp. "It's very interesting."

"Come back! There's nothing in there."

She could tell by the echo of his voice that he was following, or had at least come back as far as the overhang. Eli spoke, but all she heard was the whispering echo.

The lake looked different from here. All one could see was a mirrored surface reflecting the artificial trees and a band of sky. The cliff wall gave way to openness, and her light showed that the ramp led to a second level. "There's a cave up here," she called, and then as her light revealed more, "Half the hill is hollow!"

She walked out onto a wide floor, and as she turned and looked back, it seemed to her that she stood alone on an enormous stage, only there was water where the audience should be. She aimed her light into the wings and then upward and to the center. As far as the beam reached were arches carved into pink stone, row above row in graduated tiers. The bottom row stood some twenty feet high. Centered beneath each arch was a beige squat form of a seated quadruped, round-headed with no ears. Each wore the same benign smile on its flat-featured face. The figures had their hands or paws resting on their knees.

The right hand held a ball, the left a sheaf of grass. The place was a shrine.

"Dad? Eli? Come and see this!" The space amplified her excited shout and boomed it out with frightening volume. A rock slipped and fell and shattered on the floor, causing more echoes. When the noise died away, she could hear the jingle of the tools on Sadler's belt and the scuff of boots in sand.

"Jenny? Where are you?"

"Up here." She remembered not to shout. "Up the ramp."

"Are you hurt?"

"No. Don't yell. It causes avalanches."

"I'm coming."

Pleased with herself and her discovery, she turned and swept the light in a semicircle. As the beam passed, something moved in the center arch. She caught only a glimpse of it, something large and gray and long-haired. She jerked the light back and saw an animal in mid-spring, claws unsheathed and extended. There was no time for fear, only for one shocked thought: I'm going to be killed by a giant guinea pig. And then she tripped on a stone and fell. As she went down, her arms flew up.

The ghema's forefoot struck the light and sent it flying. A rear toe struck one of Jenny's legs, and for an instant her foot was pinned by a great weight and then released. She was aware of a richly rotten odor, the touch of fur, the sound of claws screeching on stone like giant fingernails on slate, and the animal's grunt with the impact of landing. Then, apparently realizing it had missed its target, the creature gave a deep caterwaul that soared and filled the space. The sound was round and full and velvety, and Jenny, in shock, thought: I wish Mother could have heard that—she'd really appreciate that voice. She sat up and saw the creature wheel and turn, its barrel-shaped bulk and blocky head a darkness against the gray of the opening.

"Jenny? What was that god-awful noise?" Her father called, but she didn't answer.

"If an animal gets too bold, yell at it," she remembered Eli once saying, "and if you have to, sock it on the nose, quick and hard so it knows you mean business." She couldn't see this one's nose, but she could feel and smell its breath, which was unpleasant, and she aimed two quick karate chops to the center of that airflow. On the first blow the side of her hand struck what felt like moist rubber with little prickly points embedded in it, and the second time she knew she had hit a lip because she felt it crush against a tooth and heard the animal yowl in reflex pain as it flicked its head and flung her hand back.

"Get out!" She thought she was shouting, but her voice was just a squeak. "Get out! Out! *Out!*" Her hand closed over a stone. She threw it and heard it thud against something soft, which growled. She felt for another stone and threw it too, only to hear it clatter on the floor, wide of the target. "Get out! Go 'way!" she yelled again, this time with more volume. "Get out of here!"

"What?" Sadler called. "I can't hear you. Wait a minute—we're almost there."

At that the animal growled again, and Jenny saw a shape rise in front of her. She cowered back, but instead of attacking, the shape twisted away. There was a rasp of claws, and she saw it leap onto the ramp and freeze. For a second it crouched, clearly visible in the light reflected from the pool below, light that made its eyes smolder like green coals and lit the white stripes that flanked its gray fur. She had not fully realized its size until she saw it rise on its haunches and spring out of sight. That back leg was bigger than she was.

There was loud scuffling and the jangle of a tool belt, but no voices, no outcry, and then the scuffling ended and there was total quiet. After listening a moment, she got up and nearly fell again. Her right ankle didn't want to hold her weight, and pain shot from foot to knee as she hurriedly limped over to the ramp. What she saw there frightened her still more.

Her father lay crumpled on the slope; Eli sat a few yards beyond, pressing his hand against his forehead and looking dazed. When he saw her, he simply stared and then tipped his free hand in a laconic wave.

Sadler groaned. His legs moved and he uncurled himself. "Stinking thing," he muttered, and tried to sit up. He wasn't successful on the first try, and he rearranged his long legs. "Jenny?" he asked in a conversational tone, as if a thought had just occurred to him. She limped down and knelt beside him.

"Are you badly hurt?" she asked, afraid to hear the answer. The sound of her voice startled him, and he struggled into sitting position and turned around to see her.

"Jenny? Are you all right?" he asked, and squeezed both her hands, and when she said she was, "What was that animal? Is that what you wanted to show me?"

"No—"

"Thank God!" he said illogically, and then he saw Eli sitting below them. "Did it hurt you, Eli?"

Eli turned and stared at him. "It didn't do me any good," he said.

"What happened?" Jenny asked. Her father was rubbing the back of his head, gingerly, as if feeling for damage. "Are you hurt?"

"I'm not sure." Sadler's searching hand settled on one spot. "I've got a lump back there the size of a Ping-Pong ball and growing." He brought his hand down and wiped his fingers on his pants, then sat staring dopily at the water below.

Jenny's ankle was throbbing. She wanted to sit down but was afraid if she did she couldn't stand up again, and neither her father nor Eli appeared to be in any condition to help. "Let's go back to the truck and get fixed up," she suggested and pushed herself erect. The slope of the ramp made the pain worse. "Can both of you walk?"

"What did you want to show me?" Sadler asked. "What's up there?"

"We can see it later—tomorrow."

"But what is it?"

Halfway through her description, he got up. "I want to see it now."

"She's right, sir." Eli spoke up. "I've got a cut on my head, Jenny's limping, and you're shaken up. Whatever's up there has been there a long time. It'll keep another day. Besides, the animal might decide to come back to her bed. She's not at all friendly."

"The animal—yes—" Sadler sounded as if he'd forgotten it already.

"What is that animal?" Jenny asked. "It's so big!"

"No one's ever named it," Eli said. "I've seen two others like it. Up in the mountains where it's cold. They're hunters . . ."

"Where did this one go?"

He shrugged. "I didn't watch. She probably won't come back until dark—"

"Then that gives us four hours," Sadler said. "Let's go."

TWELVE

"INTERESTING. VERY INTERESTING," WAS SADLER'S VER-
dict as he played the beam of light over the statues. "Not
only were they hi-tech, but religious as well. Or so it would
appear. I can't imagine what else this would represent,
this endless repetition on a single theme. . . ." He fell
silent as he stalked about, studying the images, setting his
torch on wide beam, focusing it again. "They don't look
particularly intelligent, do they, with those lemur eyes?
Of course this image may not represent their race but an
aspect of their deity. Perhaps all-seeing? You will notice,
Jenny—" The beam swept left, seeking her. "Jenny?" He
turned, and her name echoed out.

"Here."

The beam found her sitting on a boulder near the ramp.

"There you are. A little shaky?" Without waiting for
her answer, he went on. "You'll notice they hold a ball,
probably to represent their world, and a stalk of grain,
possibly their prime food source and therefore sacred . . .
That's something to consider, Jenny—the importance of a
specific food to a culture. We're in a very old business,
you and I, and if food were still accorded the ancient respect it deserves, I would be a high priest and you an
acolyte. We are life givers. Our work allows man to en-
dure." His light focused on the grain and then swept on.

Jenny hugged her knees and wished they'd stop shaking. Having legs limp as noodles was awkward and made
her feel foolish. It was bad enough that her ankle hurt

with every step. At the moment this whole trip seemed like a bad idea, and she was sorry she'd ever told her father to read Rothman's journal. Here he stood in a cavern, going mystical on her.

"Here." Eli handed her the torch, which had gone flying when she fell. When she let go her knees to take the light, her heels jumped and made little scuffling noises on the stone floor. "Thank you." She tried the switch, and light glared up into Eli's face. His lower lip was egg-shaped and cut. The gash on his forehead had bled down and clotted in a smeary mess in his left eyebrow.

"You don't look so hot," she said, setting the light beside her on the stone. "You want to sit down here and I'll clean you up? I've got a first-aid kit on my belt."

"Can you hold anything without dropping it?" asked Eli.

"Pretty soon. I'll quit shaking pretty soon."

He sat on the stone floor and waited trustingly. Having to worry about somebody else took her mind off her own problems, and she managed, with effort, to control her hands enough to detach and unroll the medical kit.

"I'll have to touch you," she warned him. "There's no other way to do it."

"O.K."

She took a tube of antibiotic and a swab and awkwardly but gently spread gel on his forehead and lip, let it soak to loosen the dried blood, and patted the wounds clean with gauze. "It looks worse than it is," she told him. "Does it hurt?"

"Yes," said Eli, who'd never learned the art of brave lies. He sat very still, eyes downcast, submitting to her cold fingers as she moved his face this way and that.

"O.K. Let's try some of this." She covered the cuts with liquid No-Pain. "Don't lick your lips for a while. It tastes terrible, and it'll numb your tongue so you talk funny."

"I'd rather have it hurt."

"Too late now," she said cheerfully, feeling much better now that she was being useful. With half an ear she could hear her father talking, off in one of the archways. She didn't pay much attention; both her parents had the habit of talking to themselves. They said all intelligent people did. As she waited for the anesthetic to work before she butterflied the gash, she admired Eli's perfect widow's peak, thick black lashes, and very smooth skin. Unlike with most people, the closer you got to him, the better he looked. Her grandfather had a saying: "Good-looking from far, but far from good-looking." Eli was the reverse.

"I've never done this for real before," she said, rereading the instructions on the temp-stitch pen. "Just practiced on oranges before we left home."

"Did the oranges recover?"

"My mother said they'd need a skilled cosmetic surgeon before they could risk a close-up—so I ate them."

"It's that serious?" Eli worried, wide-eyed.

"I was joking," she said quickly, and before he could get upset, she put her left hand on his forehead, pulled the gash flat, and sutured neat little "x's" across it with the pen. "That will dissolve in five days and leave no scar," she promised in her most professional manner.

"How do you know?"

"It says so on the pen." She gave him the pen to read while she painted the red line with more antibiotic. "You wait until you can see in a mirror. I did a fine job! Hold on while I stick a bandage over it to keep out the dirt."

He sat still until she said, "All done."

"I think I should tell you something," he said as he stood

up and brushed the dust off his clothes. "I didn't mind your touching."

"Thank you." She thought it was a compliment, but she wasn't sure.

"You're welcome. Where's your father?"

"Back there." She nodded over her shoulder, busy putting the things back into the first-aid kit. "Talking to himself." She snapped the kit back on her belt and stood up. Pain shot up her leg, and she bit her lip to keep from crying out.

"I don't hear him," Eli said. "I don't see his light."

"He's probably in one of the alcoves. Dad?" she called into the dimness, and the cavern echoed the word. "Dad? Where are you?"

"Dr. Sadler?"

"Dad?"

They stood waiting for the echoes to die so they could hear. Sadler didn't answer. Jenny felt a cold spot form in her stomach. It would be a relief to cry, she thought, but that didn't seem fair to Eli. Instead she turned on her wrist-phone page and waited. And waited.

"Dad?"

"Let's go look."

"O.K." She started after Eli. The pain of walking made her half sick, but she persisted. It would either get worse or she'd get used to it.

From where Sadler had stood talking about the grain, they followed his bootprints across a stretch of sand to where the floor was bare again. Each arch looked like the one before; a plump, big-eyed quadruped stared benignly into space seated atop a fluted cupcake pedestal. They seemed to be smiling, but it was difficult to tell if the

U-shaped groove below their eyes was nose or mouth.

"Have you ever seen anything like them before?" she asked Eli.

"No. Have you?"

Since he lived on Tanin and had seen considerably more of this world than she had, she thought his question odd, but she answered, "No," politely and limped around a pedestal to see if anything was back there. She found two high arched openings. One led into the pedestal, the other into a gallery behind it. The inner gallery was also filled with statues. The discovery made the cold knot expand in her stomach. She flashed the light up into the interior of the statue.

"What did you do? Its eyes lit up!" Eli came running.

"Shone my light inside. The statues are hollow.

"He could be anywhere," she said, showing Eli the inner gallery. "He probably went exploring by himself. He likes to do that sort of thing."

"Then you should go back to the truck and get that boot off." He stepped past her and led the way outside. After a last look at the passageways, she followed, reluctantly.

"If he's O.K., why doesn't he answer the page?" she wondered aloud.

"Maybe it won't transmit through stone. Did you ever try it?"

"No," she admitted, looking up at the tiers, hoping to see a light moving somewhere. All was still and dark. "Dad?" she called. "We're going back to the truck." The statues stared into the dimness, listening with her to the echoes.

Jenny and Eli had almost reached the ramp when she heard, or thought she heard, Sadler shout, "No!" and a diminishing echo of "oh-oh-oh."

"Dad? Where are you?"

"What is it?" Eli whispered.

"Sh! Listen."

"What are we listening for?" Eli whispered again after a minute had passed.

"I heard him call. I'm sure I did. We'd better find him," she whispered, and started back into the cavern.

"No!" Eli refused. "That's not the rules. The rules are I don't take chances. That's how I stay alive alone."

"You won't help me look?"

"I won't help us get lost. You wait here. I'll run back to the truck and get my cave rope and—"

"Cave rope?"

"A white lifeline. You secure one end at the entrance to the cave and uncoil it as you go so you can find your way out again."

"Like Theseus in the Minotaur's labyrinth."

"What?"

"It doesn't matter. I don't want to wait, Eli. What if that giant guinea pig comes back and it's still in a filthy temper?"

She turned and limped back along the arches. Eli reached out as if to stop her, then shook his head. "If you're lost when I get back, don't expect me to come looking for you!"

"I won't," she promised. She had no intention of getting lost.

She went back to where they'd left off searching and checked each pedestal and door until she came to one where the statue had fallen and lay in pieces on the floor. A well-worn path had been trampled through the shards and stone dust. On the path were bootprints.

She followed them into the archway opening and found

a huge corridor leading straight back into the cliff. It was as large as the tunnel under The Wall, and her first thought was to wonder if the same people were responsible for this. The place was as dark as a mine shaft.

"Dad?" His bootprints ended with the sand. The stone floor was dark with an old grease stain. The air smelled rancid. "Dad?" She tried the page again and got no answer.

The cold knot in her stomach spread and pushed up against her lungs. If she didn't think about it she could hear herself breathing. She limped into the corridor, light bobbing up and down, and edged over to the wall, feeling safer with one flank protected. That way she only had to look ahead, behind, and on one side.

Some twenty yards down was an archway with bad breath. The floor was extra dirty here and littered with things she didn't want to look at too closely.

"Dad? Are you in there?"

Whispering scuffs and scurryings, squeaks, and little snarls echoed out of the dark hole. She aimed the beam inside. Small red eyes gleamed, living garnets that fired and fled. Something with lots of legs hurried down her arm. She mashed it with a slap. With a glance back at the arch of gray light where she'd entered, she took a deep breath and made herself cross the corridor for a better view.

It had been a spacious, vaulted hall. The walls were covered with faded murals of a fantastic landscape. The ceiling was a pink sky with clouds. What looked like ruined machines stood on raised pedestals, all thick with dust and filth. Pieces of dry fur hides crackled beneath her boots, and with every step she crushed bones scattered on blue tile. On a platform at the far end of the room was a mound of dry grass, shaped into an unkempt bed. Below it lay the gutted body of a grazer. Small furred scavengers crawled over the carcass, feeding. She had never seen an animal in that condition. She knew it happened but had never wanted to think about it. Alien animals didn't eat people. She was fairly sure of that. Still . . . she searched the big room thoroughly with her light. Her father wasn't there.

THIRTEEN

IN THE CORRIDOR AGAIN, SHE FOUGHT THE URGE TO RUN to daylight and green living things, to leave this dark and dirty place. Instead, she went on searching.

"Da-ad! Where are you? Answer me!"

"Me! Me! Me!" insisted the echoes.

There were other, smaller rooms, empty, as if nothing dared or wished to share this place with the hunter. The passage ended at a pair of ramps curving down like Siamese connectors. She stopped, uncertain which side to choose.

The floor was windswept by a constant draft. A noise made her jump and flatten back against the wall. A small, pale-furred creature scurried past, squeaking to itself. Just beyond light range a shadow moved.

"Dad?"

It stopped, or seemed to, and she thought she saw a big head turn to look at her, but no eyes reflected light. Hair stood up on her arms, and the back of her neck itched with nerves. What if that big animal had a mate?

"Is that you, Dad?"

Light digits on her wristband showed that Eli had been gone less than fifteen minutes. It took that long to walk back to the truck. So if she was in trouble, she couldn't count on help from him. She set the torch on long beam. There was nothing down there. Of course, if it was stalking her it might have stepped into a doorway. . . . A little whimper of fear escaped at that idea and surprised her. She hadn't realized she was quite that frightened.

She took a deep breath, returned the light to wide beam, and set off down the right-hand ramp. If she only made right turns, all she'd have to do to find her way back up again was make left turns.

Walking on the slope was painful; her foot protested all this use, and she had to keep touching the wall for balance. The wall had bugs.

The ramp angled right, then left, then right again in an inverted Z. At the far end of the Z was daylight. She limped toward that welcome sight and came out into a vast round chamber cut from the living rock and lit by opaque stone panels ribbed into walls and ceiling. Fifty feet from where she stood was another entrance, the exit from the left ramp.

The arena floor was like a beige pool carved from stone, a pool into which a pebble had been thrown, causing ripple rings. In the center of the rings sat her father, his back to her, the page on his wrist phone beeping small drips of sound into the silence. To regain her poise, she paused and clipped her torch back onto her belt. The sound of the beeper made her shiver. Why didn't he answer? Why was he sitting there like that? Could you still sit up if you were dead?

"Dad?" she called. He gave no sign of having heard. A sharp pain jabbed her stomach. If she could hear his beeper, he could hear her voice. She shut off the page. "I've been hunting all over for you. Why didn't you answer? What's wrong?"

When he still didn't respond, she started over the stone ripples toward him, only to see him turn as if seated on a swivel. He was sitting in the same position as the statues, hands resting palm-up on each knee, empty, as was his expression.

"You should not come here. You are damaged." He was whispering in his computer voice, and the words carried as if he were shouting. "Only the whole may enter. Only the true resound. The imperfect clank and tonkle like cracked bells, badly cast."

She stopped still on the third ridge and barely breathed, so scared that she wanted to faint. He wasn't playing. There was something very wrong. He didn't even look like himself, his face all taut, teeth clenched. She remembered overhearing her mother say once, "What would you do if you suddenly suspected someone you loved had gone insane? You wouldn't want to believe it. You'd find excuses for them. If it was a stranger, you'd see clearly and take precautions to protect yourself."

"Why didn't you answer your beeper?"

"You interrupt the music!"

She listened. All she could hear was silence. She let more minutes pass. He didn't move.

"Let's get out of here, Dad," she said quietly. "Let's go back to the truck. You got a bad blow when you hit your head. We'll—"

"Listen!"

"We've got to get out of here! The animal might come back—"

"Leave me in peace!" He shouted, this man who never shouted, who seldom showed anger. "Can't you understand? I want to hear my music! Get out!"

She nearly ran; comrade and protector had become enemy. For a long dreadful moment he glared at her; then his expression changed as if he heard something new in the silence. He turned away with an eerie lack of effort.

Her knees went wobbly, and she sat down on the ridge to consider possibilities while she kept an eye on him. The most obvious conclusion was concussion. But would it make you act like this? She dismissed that. Or was he playing? She dismissed that, too.

As quietly as she could, she checked her first-aid kit to see if it contained anything that might help. Tranquilizers? But how would she get him to take a capsule? As she thought about it, she realized she was afraid to get that near him. Anti-traum? She could toss a capsule to him—if he'd use it. But somehow she didn't think his problem was physical. She put the kit away and stood up.

"This isn't my idea of a treasure hunt," she said, "watching you pretend you're some stupid statue." She waited to see if that would goad him into normal movement. When it didn't she tried another tack. "I'm going back to the truck and call the port and have the paramedics come and get you. You're not well, and I don't know how to help you."

She got as far as the trough of the second ripple before flickers in the light level made her look back. Her father was glitching. There was no other word for it; his form was shifting and spreading, then retracting in spasmodic jerks. His head elongated into a baseball bat, sank back to normal, squashed flat and wide—and then he disappeared as if he'd been switched off. There was a dimple in the stone where he'd been sitting.

"Holography?" she whispered, almost as relieved as she had been terrified. She was searching the ceiling, looking for hidden equipment, when a column of pale brown smoke or gas rose from the dimple-like depression. A brown image formed in the mist, vaguely human at first, before the head and chest grew bulbous, and clawed, chitinous arms gleamed in the light. She watched the thing grow until it was taller than James Sadler, and she began backing away and fell on her rump. Fear made pain unimportant and gave her the impetus to scramble over the last ripple to the flat aisle where she could run. If the figures were only pictures, projections, they would stay where they were. But if they were something else—

She looked back. The thing looked like a huge weird ant standing on its hind legs. What she'd first taken to be arms was an antenna on its clam-shaped head. The antenna moved via socket and ball joint, she noted, and then giggled at the timing of her observation. At her laugh the thing turned toward her. She stopped laughing. It had shiny black raspberry eyes with spines between the segments. In place of lips and teeth, flippers with serrated edges folded across the mouth. There were spines all over its body.

It's a magnification, she thought; it's not real. It's part of some sort of security system to scare people away. Insects can't walk upright, can't grow this big. She was trying to remember from biophysics the law that proved her right when another ant appeared in the exit behind her, just as large, and walking properly, headed straight toward her.

Her scream was quite distinct. There was no echo; the arena's acoustics were perfect. The blur in the sound of her running footsteps was caused by her limp.

She was about to run out the other exit when she saw something moving toward her in the half-light, pinpoints of shine on a lacquer-smooth body. With a sound between a yelp and a moan she wheeled, too frightened to think of more than escape. If she ran around the circle ahead of them, she could reach the exits again before they did. Unless they had friends, of course.

But they're not real, her reason insisted. They make no sound, have no smell. She glanced over her shoulder; the second illusion was gaining on her, the third was speeding up. Only the one in the center ring seemed content to watch.

Halfway around the arena she saw the crest of the outermost ripple was getting higher. This aisle didn't encircle the arena but sloped down to a curve beneath it. There was no way now to get back to the exits.

Each step on the right foot pounded pain up her leg. She tried using only the ball of the foot, but that threw her off balance, and so she forced herself to run normally until the muscles could take no more punishment and gave way beneath her weight. She fell and rolled against the outer wall and for an instant lay still, preoccupied by pain. Then she thought how it might feel to be bitten by a mouth like that and sat up. As quickly as she did, something clamped around her right arm, then her left, and she was hoisted up, feet dragging, and lugged forward.

For a second she was too shocked to struggle and could only stare. She was being carried by an ant on either side. To turn her head brought her eyes within inches of their heads and a bulging berry eye with its protective spikes. To allow her body to touch any point of those heads meant being punctured by spines. What if they decided to make a wish?

She wanted very much to faint but couldn't. After the first terrible fear all she felt was a curious detachment. She knew what was happening, but it no longer seemed to matter. She was being carried off by giant insects who smelled of oil and had mouth flippers folded up like blinders. Her leg hurt and her shoulders and both knees. The one hand she could see was scraped and bleeding from her latest fall—but that was how things were. A curious peace came over her.

As they dragged her down the ramp, she looked up at the outer wall. It really was quite beautiful, she thought; highly polished panes of petrified wood set between the natural stone pillars. How clever of them. Eli would appreciate this.

A warm breeze blew up the ramp and ruffled her hair. The floor was covered with sand. Her feet were dragging through it, and she could hear small creaking sounds like footsteps on cold snow. Ant feet. She would like to see snow now, white and cold and pure.

There was an opening in the wall; the smell of sun-baked rocks, and from somewhere the sound of a bird. She focused on that sound. They carried her to the opening and dropped her. As she fell, she thought of her ant farm, long ago, on another world—they were cleaning trash out of the nest, garbage detail. She was garbage tumbling down a cliff of hot sand.

FOURTEEN

WHEN SHE FINALLY STOPPED SLIDING, A SMALL AVA-lanche of sand and pebbles rushed past as if she were a boulder in their stream. The bird sang on, unconcerned.

Gradually she roused herself enough to sit up and look back at the hole, expecting to see hideous faces peering down. But there were no faces. There was no hole. There was only a rounded hill of ribbed sandstone eroding down into ridges and pinnacles. Even her slide trail was obscured by the mini-avalanche.

Maybe I'm the one who lost my mind, she thought—so scared I imagined things? But giant ants? The pain in her shoulders was real, and the scuff on her hand. She took off her jacket to check her arms. The jacket was dirty and ripped in six places. Her wrist phone was gone. A ragged scratch marked where the band used to be. Both arms were red and pinch-bruised from elbow to shoulder.

The ants weren't hallucinations. Was her father? But he didn't bear thinking about now—or Eli, who was probably searching for them both, walking those black halls and calling, forgetting his rules.

As she shook the jacket to straighten out the sleeves, she caught a whiff of oil and remembered: the ants' heads smelled like that. They must be machines, computerized things, but whose, and for what purpose? And why didn't they oust the guinea pig down the hall? Why her? Not that understanding would make much difference at the moment. "I've got to find the truck and call for help," she said aloud, and was shaken to hear how weak she sounded out here in the open.

Standing up took effort. Her right leg wanted to crumple. Downslope was a stunted tree. She managed to break off a branch to use as a walking stick. She felt bad about breaking the tree; it was having a hard enough time as it was.

All she had to do now was to get back to the truck. From what she could remember of the view when they landed, she thought she was on the other side of the cliff behind the pool, in an eroded valley. To the right should be the desert slope that stretched to The Wall; left would take her back, around the hill to where the airtrucks were parked. It seemed simple enough, a three-mile walk—five at the most.

Two hours later she was detouring along a gully too steep to traverse and too wide to jump, forced steadily away from the direction she wanted to take and no longer sure quite where she was. Trees obscured the view. She was sore and tired and hungry and not very far from panic.

Her father was right, she thought, sitting on a log to rest; travel was educational. Without this trip she'd have never known how scared she could get, or how much she could hurt and still walk. If she were at home, her ankle alone would be good for bed and sympathy. The arm bruises would frighten everyone—especially her mother. All four of the grandparents would fuss and send over their physicians . . . but she wasn't home. And she wasn't going to get there at this rate.

Leaves rustled in the brush nearby, and a trio of potoos filed into view. She had never seen them at such close range, and they shocked her. They were ostrich-sized, and their feet looked powerful enough to remind her of a line in one of her books: "When cornered, an ostrich's kick can disembowel a horse."

She watched them disappear among the trees and marveled at how well their variegated browns blended with the landscape. Even their orange feet fitted in, matching dead leaves on creeper vines, several flowers, and mushrooms. When the birds stood still you couldn't be sure you saw them.

Since they were going in the general direction she wanted to go, she waited until they had disappeared and then limped after them. She found an animal trail worn deep with use and age. The path looped around the gully's end and meandered up a hill where stone slabs lay in parallel lines on either side. It switchbacked down to a natural cave and wound around outcroppings.

She was trudging up a slope in the dusk, intent on keeping her footing in a stretch of gravel, when a thick-tailed, bushy-haired creature the size of a sheep came hurrying over the trail, head down, lost in its own shaggy thoughts. Each saw the other only on collision, and both gave startled cries of fear. She fell, and the creature was knocked sideways by the impact. For a moment the creature stared in round-eyed amazement and then turned tail and fled.

Another time she would have laughed to see that shocked expression on a furry face, but now the jarring fall shook the last of her reserve and she sat there in the dust and cried. Once started, she couldn't stop.

The sobs gradually wore down to hiccupping shudders. The stars came out. In the trees downhill, insects sang, but around her all was quiet, as if everything were listening. But then, she thought, if she heard an alien animal crying outside her window at home, she'd be still and listen too.

In her muff pocket she found a battered tissue among fragments of stone. She threw the stones away, blew her nose, and felt better; the tears had washed something heavy from her soul. With the help of the torch she found her stick, got back on her feet, and started off again.

The torchlight made a tunnel of the path. To remind herself there was no roof above, she would aim the beam up at the stars or sweep it from side to side. Once, the light picked up a big night bird gliding silently above the hills. She watched it, envious of its ability to fly, until the bird beat its long wings and soared up beyond the range of the intrusive beam.

Then from the east came a high thin whine, like that of a huge mosquito. Three stars came speeding over the hills. A shaft of light shot down from the central star and swept the crest of the ridge.

"Eli!" she called, as if he could hear. She waved the torch and nearly dropped it in excitement. The searchlight beam raced down across the valley, pushing a circle of colors through the darkness, sending shadows out in fingers that shortened as the light moved on. "Here, Eli! Eli? Come back! Eli!"

Maybe it wasn't him? Only lights were visible, not the actual truck. For all she knew, it was a miner looking for a place to camp and hunt petrified wood. The lights circled, and she waved her torch until her arm ached and burned. The searchlight swept up the slope and over her. Motor pitch changed; the craft banked and slowed to hover overhead. Red flashing landing lights came on. She limped to the tree line to give the pilot landing room. The spotlight followed her, then went off with the motor.

The warped hatch sang *"boink!"* as it opened, and Jenny grinned. Eli stood framed by the cabin light, peering out into the darkness. "I'm so glad to see you!"

"It's a pretty night," he said as she limped to meet him. "A good night for a walk. You said you weren't going to get lost."

"I'm not *lost.*" She was in no mood for sarcasm if that was what he intended. She was going to hug him but changed her mind. "Did you find my father?"

"He wasn't lost either."

"Where is he?"

"Sleeping in your truck."

He was safe. She stared up at Eli, as puzzled as she was relieved. "Sleeping? Wasn't he worried about me?"

"He was asleep when I came back from hunting you both. I don't know how or when he came back. I couldn't waken him."

"Does he look . . . normal?"

"Better than you." He jumped down to help her into the truck.

"Ouch!" She flinched away as he grasped her arm. "Don't help. I can get in by myself." He frowned but stepped aside to watch as she got in by sitting on the hatchway, scooting back, turning around, and hoisting herself onto the spare seat.

"You're very dirty," he observed as he slid into the pilot's seat.

"Does that mean you want me to sit on the floor?"

"No. It means you're very dirty." He closed the hatch and turned on the motor.

"How did you know where I was?"

"I didn't. Not until I saw little light beams jabbing the dark above the cliff."

"Did you hunt us a long time?"

"Yes."

"What did you find?"

"You weren't there."

There were times, Jenny thought, when she'd like to shake him until his teeth rattled. The truck lifted off, and at a thousand feet she saw she had been right in her guess as to where she was. Lights on the Sadler truck were visible from here, the only light in miles of darkness.

"What did you find?" Eli asked. She told him. By the time she'd finished, they had landed. "Do you believe me?" she asked as they walked to her truck. "I know it doesn't sound real, but it was. It happened. That's how I got outside."

"I'm never sure what's real," he said. "I just watch and listen and hope. The pale blue ship that radar never sees is as real to me as Dr. Rule—and I've seen her often. I don't think people know what's real; they just pretend. What's an ant?"

She stared at him, confused, and then took refuge in his question. There were no ants on Tanin. "I'll draw you a picture after I've seen Dad."

"And after you take a bath." He caught her expression and added, "You don't look like Jenny dirty. You're out of character."

Her father was sleeping normally, or so it seemed to her. The only odd thing was that instead of opening his bed he had fallen asleep in the pilot's seat, as if that were the first thing he'd reached before collapsing. He snored as if he'd walked a hundred miles that day. She stared down at his face, trying to dismiss the image she'd seen in the arena, the cold stranger to whom she meant nothing.

"He's all right," Eli said from the hatch behind her.

"How did he get so tired?"

"How did you?"

"Fear?" she whispered.

"And the music."

"There wasn't any music!" she said, irked. "I couldn't hear a sound. And that wasn't him—just his image."

"The music was as real to him as his image was to you, I think," said Eli. "As real as your ants. Earth-born people expect everything to follow Earth's rules. But you can't give human explanations to inhuman things. Earth rules aren't the rules of the people who left these ruins. What we see and hear may be remnants of their past time, lingering patterns of low-level energy provoked by our presence."

"Ghosts?" said Jenny. "Are you saying we're stirring up ghosts?"

"You could call them that. It's not correct, but you could call them that."

"Ghosts don't leave bruises."

"No." He glanced out the door as if wanting to leave or at least change the subject. "Do you need help getting your boots off?"

His expression told her he wasn't going to say anything more about ghosts, and she was too worn out to argue. "Please," she said, sitting down and sticking out a leg.

They had to cut the right boot off.

FIFTEEN

TO AVOID THE CHANCE OF FALLING AGAIN, SHE SAT ON the floor of the shower to bathe. The soap made every scratch burn. In her candy-stripe nightshirt she came out of the dressing room to find her bed open and Eli sitting on the end, a brown mug in each hand.

"Thank you," she whispered, settling gratefully against the pillow and stretching out her legs.

"You don't know what it is yet." He handed her a mug.

"I meant thanks for the bed. And for hunting us, and finding me, and—"

"Beef stew." He fished two spoons from a pocket and stuck one into her mug.

"You're right," she agreed after tasting the stuff. Hungry as she was, the stew seemed a freeze-dried gourmet's delight, savory, hot, satisfying. By the time the mug was empty she was half asleep. She was aware of his taking the mug away and a blanket settling over her, soft and warm. "I have to draw you the ants," she said, "so you'll recognize them. They're not really ants, but . . ."

"Tomorrow."

The lights above her head went off, and she heard him cross over to the galley and wash the mugs. She was going to ask him if he'd mind staying with her for a while when she passed out.

Sometime in the night she wakened from a dream of home and sat up in surprise at seeing the dimly lit cabin instead of her room. Eli lay asleep on the floor, hood up, hands clasped over his belt buckle, mouth open in an "O" like a porcelain singing angel. She stared down at him, wondering what his lips would look like gilded, and realized what had wakened her was the quiet. Her father had stopped snoring; there wasn't a sound from outside, not even the wind.

She slid down to the end of the bed to avoid tripping on Eli and hobbled over to make sure Sadler was still breathing. She didn't ask herself why she thought he might not be. He had shifted position and lay as curled as it was possible for someone his size to curl in those cradle pilot seats, knees drawn up, one hand tucked beneath his cheek, the other clenched at his waist. He needed a shave, and in this light white hairs gleamed at his temples. She'd never noticed those before. Or the crow's-feet. His chest swelled with a slow deep breath and sank again. She waited for the next few breaths, wanting to be sure, then turned to go back to bed.

Something brushed against the truck, twice and then again, a raspy wire-brush sound that came from below. But how would an animal get under there at night? The electrical charge from the security system was more than strong enough to frighten animals away.

The truck rocked as something heavy walked up the ramp and scratched against the door like long hard fingernails trying to open a can. No one had remembered to turn on the security system! She leaned across Sadler and hit the button on the control panel. A series of green lights blinked on.

From underneath the truck came a sharp explosive hiss, like a shuttle's air brakes. The cabin went completely dark, then shook. Through windows on the hatch side she saw what looked like ball lightning float toward the pool, touch a jade tree, and disappear. The tree hummed like a giant harp and went still again.

"Intruders have been expelled from within the security perimeter," the computer murmured. "Cabin lights have been turned off for added security. Please maintain silence."

What's out there? Jenny wondered, and felt a sudden urge to go to the bathroom—but that seemed an awkward place to be in case disaster struck. Discipline, her mother said, saw one through any situation. She considered waking her father and then decided not to, not yet. Suppose he talked in that computer voice?

Eli stirred but didn't waken, or if he did, didn't say anything. She edged closer to the window. At first all she could see was a few stars and a cloud bank moving in from the west. Eli's truck was a shadow darker than the ground around it, as were the jade trees.

Then, at the edge of the pool, a large blackness began to move, slowly, and then another, walking upright, or seeming to. Ants? Maybe with those eyes they could see through one-way glass? She pictured them standing up on their hind legs, peering in the windows. But were they big enough to be ants?

If she pressed the emergency autopilot button to take them back to port, how angry would her father be when he woke up and found out?

The outside lights came on. There was no animal near the truck. Cabin lighting returned and with it her ability to breathe freely again. She watched until her leg began to ache from standing. Nothing moved in the circle of light outside. Puzzled and uneasy, she went back to bed. As she drifted off to sleep again, a single lightning flare lit up the valley. Thunder rumbled and died away.

She was wakened in the morning by Sadler whistling as he shaved. Eli was nowhere in sight. The sky was overcast and cold. The cabin smelled of lemon soap, and orange juice tablets dissolving in the galley—normal morning sounds and smells, familiar and reassuring. She stretched and winced as her right foot rammed into a fold of blanket. Her arm bruises were dark blue and purplish-red with yellow-green around the edges. I look like I'm rotting, she thought, and pulled her sleeves down so no one would notice.

When the dressing room door slid open, she closed her eyes, wanting to observe Sadler before he knew she was awake. He tiptoed past her bunk and paused, then went on to the galley. Food packets rustled; cabinet doors opened and shut softly; the table panel hummed as it slid out. Coffee aromatics joined the orange and lemon. Through the quivering fringe of her lashes he looked as normal as the morning. She feigned waking up.

"Hello," he said. "How are you?" He sounded sane again.

"Hungry." That was true and noncommittal. "How are you?"

"I saw your arms." He glanced up from measuring water for the powdered eggs. "And your ants. I thought I'd had a nightmare until I talked with Eli. We had—what is for him—quite a chat. What he told me of your adventure, combined with the fact that the last thing I clearly remember about yesterday is seeing you putting a patch on his head, tends to shake me up a bit. Whatever you saw and spoke with, it wasn't me. I'm so sorry you were frightened." The blender whirred and shut off.

"You don't remember how you got back here? Where you were?"

He shook his head. "Just vague bits, images—I don't know what we're dealing with." He took six biscuit pellets from a bag and dropped them into water. "We'll have breakfast, and then I'll take you back to the port hospital."

"All I have is a sprain and bruises," she said. "What can medics do for that except have me rest?"

"Are you sure?" He didn't quite manage to conceal the relief in his voice. "Those bruises look painful."

"Ugly, too. Where did you see the ants?"

"Somewhere in there—I don't know. As I said, I thought it was a nightmare until I talked with Eli. . . ." He turned and busied himself at the stove. Jenny, watching, wondered why she didn't quite believe him. Perhaps he'd been so frightened he didn't want to remember?

"Where is Eli?"

"Out for a swim and a change of clothes. He found scratch marks on the hatch and got all worked up about the perfection of the finish being destroyed. I suspect it was your furry friend from the cavern, paying us a visit while we were out yesterday."

She didn't say anything, not wanting to scare him more.

Half an hour later the three of them sat talking over breakfast, or rather the Sadlers talked and Eli ate and listened.

"It's possible what happened could be due to gas," Sadler speculated. "That hill is honeycombed with chambers—like an abandoned mine. Gas may seep out of the stone and hang in the air. We breathed it—and had hallucinations."

"I don't believe that," she said bluntly.

"You might have been bruised when that pushy animal jumped you; shock does funny things—you don't remember clearly. As for the oil, those thorn bushes out there with the waxy leaves smell like your jacket. You walked through them yesterday."

"Why would we both hallucinate ants?"

"Yes. Good point," he conceded.

"And why didn't Eli see them?"

"Circumstance? Luck?"

"Or we did something to attract them. Like use our wrist phones."

"You paged me . . . but the energy involved is so minute. . . ." Sadler fell silent, puzzling over the matter.

She watched Eli split his biscuit and butter one perfect half. As with everything he did, he was totally absorbed. With the precise care of a portrait painter putting the highlight in an eye, he applied a minute dab of grape jelly to the biscuit's middle, held the morsel to the light to appreciate its brown and gold and gemmy purple, then took a careful bite. The swelling on his lip was down, but the spot was obviously still sore. Seeing her watching, he blushed and had difficulty swallowing. She was sorry she embarrassed him.

"You don't talk much during meals," she observed.

"No."

"Why not?"

"Because that's when I eat."

"Oh. What do you think we should do?"

"Finish breakfast and leave. Go explore somewhere else."

"Are you two trying to convince me that whoever abandoned this place left behind guard drones that still function?" Sadler asked. "That we accidentally activated a security system with our wrist phones?"

"It could be," said Jenny. "Eli has never seen the ants. He doesn't wear any electronic gear. And we haven't seen them outside. Maybe they're programmed to stay within a map?"

"Or time," said Eli, and confused her. "I don't know what they are, but they weren't here before."

"And now?" Sadler asked, and Jenny shivered at the answer.

"There is something else here. Something that thinks. Other than us. Every living thing creates waves in the world around it—like ripples of energy. . . ." He saw the way they were looking at him. "You don't feel that?"

"No . . . but I think you might," Jenny said, intrigued by the idea. "You see, we've spent our lives surrounded by people, millions of them. Any instinctive sensitivity we might have had like that shorted out from overload, but I've read Australian aborigines could follow a fifty-year-old trail by touching the trees and rocks the men they tracked had touched. Bushmen in the Kalahari could feel land vehicles approaching days away. We once could smell rain in the wind and feel the tension of earthquakes waiting to happen. Yes, I believe you—without understanding why. Do you think we're in real danger?"

"Yes."

SIXTEEN

"ARE YOU GOING TO LEAVE?"

"We're not." Sadler spoke before the boy could answer her. "This is exactly the sort of place I hoped to find. I've come too far to be put off by imagination run amuck. Whatever occupies this ruin, it's nothing supernatural." He rose and began clearing the breakfast table, his expression indicating that he considered the matter settled. "You will spend the day in bed, resting that foot, and I'm going out to where we were headed yesterday, before we got sidetracked in the cave. Coming with me, Eli?" Eli hesitated, looking from Jenny's face to her father's, then nodded with no enthusiasm. "Good! I'll call Dr. Bower and report in while you get the bikes ready. No sense walking more than we have to."

She noticed he didn't mention their misadventures to Dr. Bower. But then Bower already disapproved of this trip.

"If you're not back by three or don't answer your page, I'm calling the port and sending the emergency patrol for you," she warned Sadler as he was leaving. "I'm not joking. And I don't think it's fair to ask Eli to go with you just because he feels he hasn't earned his guide fee."

He paused in the hatchway and looked back at her. She'd never used this tone with him and wasn't sure of his reaction. "Don't fuss," he said mildly. "We'll be fine."

She watched them ride away and felt left behind. This trip wasn't fun any more, if it ever had been. Common sense told her it wasn't wise to stay here; not only was it pointless to risk danger for a lark, it was also selfish. If something happened to them . . .

She stirred and stretched, made uneasy by the route her thoughts were taking. Sometimes it didn't pay to be too aware. An animal bleated somewhere nearby. She sat up to look out, and the little hill that contained the horned turtle's den caught her eye. Eli said the den had a blue tile floor—which might be worth seeing—and going out was better than sitting here getting depressed. Before leaving the truck, she put a gun in her muff pocket and stopped at the freight bay to get a few tools.

The outside air was cool and damp and smelled of plants. Animals looked up when they saw her, curious, but none approached, which was just as well. Her confidence wasn't all it had been, after yesterday.

All she could see of the den was a hole in the hillock beneath a slab of sandstone. A worn path led to the burrow. If Eli hadn't told her about the tile, she wouldn't have noticed the blue fragments here and there, half covered by dirt. Air coming from the burrow mouth smelled musky.

"I'm not crawling in there," she announced to no one in particular, and sat down to rest her foot. The curve of river to the south looked cold in this gray light. After a moment there was a scratching, scrambling sound, and an animal emerged from the burrow. It blinked against the cloud glare as they eyed each other. The size of a large badger, with a stubby horn on its nose, it had short thick legs with heavy claws and wore a knobby brown shell several sizes too large, as if it had grabbed the first one it saw on its way out. Unlike earthly turtles, this creature wore fine dark fur beneath its shell and had big brown eyes.

/132

"Hello," she said. The turtle hissed. "You weren't expecting visitors?" The creature hissed again. It had no teeth, just hard purple gums. She wondered if it bit. Eli said the turtles ate potoo eggs and baby potoos—which meant that toothless mouth might possess formidable gumming power.

With no warning the turtle jumped, stiff-legged, and clanked its shell against the sandstone. Jenny grabbed pebbles to throw in its face if it attacked, then saw the turtle had other problems. It was desperately trying to scratch its left hind leg at a spot no claw could reach. It tried to bite the leg but couldn't stretch far enough out of its shell. A second jump didn't satisfy, nor did repeated vigorous shakings. The shakings, however, revealed the source of the irritation. Where the leg emerged from the bottom shell, just above the knee, was a fold of bare skin. In that fold was a thimble-sized shiny black thing with a lot of legs.

"Hold still," she told the animal, as if it could understand, and she reached out with the trowel and scraped the bug off in one neat swipe. The turtle gave a little yelp and pulled into its shell. The horn closed up the head hole. Claws barred the other four.

Not wanting to upset the animal further, she scooted a few yards over to search for the blue tile. Some six inches down, her trowel struck a solid layer. She scraped away until a small patch of sand and dirt had been removed, then used the whisk broom to dust the surface clean. What looked like ice-blue lucite or glass gleamed there, so hard that when she used her hand and then her sleeve to polish, she found the surface unscratched. Embedded in the floor was an etching, a white stylized image of one of the creatures sculpted in the cavern. It was wearing a halo.

"Whee-chuk-chuk-chuk!" something nearby comment-ed in an oddly juicy voice. Absorbed in digging, she'd forgotten the turtle and glanced up to find it standing be-side her, almost nose to nose. She quickly leaned away; it had a distinct body odor.

"Interesting, isn't it?" she said, not wanting to hurt its feelings by letting it know she thought it stank. "They're wearing halos. Do you think that means they were holy? Or is that a symbol of psychic energy radiating from their heads?"

"Chuk-chuk!"

"You may be right—they just had terrible taste in hats." As she said the word "hats," she suddenly knew what she was seeing—the halo was an amplifier.

Her first impulse was to call her father and tell him the news, then she hesitated. She was supposed to be resting safely in the truck, not out here digging, all alone. He might not be too pleased to learn she'd disobeyed. Re-minded of her own carelessness, she stood up and looked around for danger.

A small herd of grazers were down along the riverbank, some drinking, others feeding. Their sentry barked; all heads raised and turned to look at her, the unknown ele-ment. Among a grove of trees like giant Queen Anne's lace, browsers fed, hidden by foliage. She could hear leaves ripping and branches breaking as the animals moved. Birds or insects gave intermittent calls. A furry black animal nosed around Eli's truck. There was nothing that looked frightening, and yet . . .

She looked down at that patch of ancient floor, at the benign, alien face with its odd hearing aid, and wondered what they had listened to, or for, in this valley where their cities had come and gone so long ago that wilderness had come again. She gathered up her tools and limped back toward the trucks.

"Wheech?" inquired the turtle, scrambling after her.

"You don't have to follow me. I'm no Androcles—and you're certainly no lion." The turtle ignored her and followed right along. Reaching the truck, it hurried up the ramp ahead of her and stood in front of the door. There was no way she could enter without the turtle's going in first. If she'd had two good feet, she would have taken the chance of shoving it away, but since keeping her balance was an effort, she decided not to risk the chance of further injury, like getting her leg gummed.

"Surprise," she said. "I'm not going in. Not yet, anyway." She opened the freight bay, where they'd packed the box with the blue glass amplifiers, and took one out. The turtle's claws clicked on the ramp as it came down to investigate, then tried to take the package from her.

"Eli never said you turtles were this pesty. Why don't you go hunt bugs, or take a bath, or find someone else to bother?"

"Wheech?"

"Out!" she ordered firmly, pointing toward the pool. The turtle looked at her, then at her outstretched hand, and plodded off, head down, muttering soft "chuks" to itself. The quickness of its seeming understanding made her pause and feel rather guilty until she remembered how easily the family dogs could con her.

The amplifier had been wrapped securely in bubble bags, and it took her some time to open them. With the fragile piece in her hands she hesitated, remembering the pain wearing it had caused before. But if she didn't experiment, she'd never know what they heard here.

She put the thing, bowl-down, atop her head, turned

around to face the pool, and cautiously slid the amplifier back into position.

At first all she heard was silence amplified, the rounded steady hiss of a seashell, or deep space. Then somewhere a bird sang, three notes so sweet and clear that she got goose bumps. She was turning to find the singer when there was a deafening hiss. She snatched the amplifier off her head. The airtruck's hatch was sliding open.

SEVENTEEN

THERE IN THE HATCH STOOD A THING, DARK-FURRED AND tall, with round pale lemur eyes that studied her in cold malevolence. The shock of recognition took her breath in a whispered, "Ohhh!" Now she knew what had scratched on the door, recognized the dark forms moving in the night. This was the living version of the statues in the shrine, the reality and not the ideal. There was nothing gentle or benign about this one.

The smiling curve that suggested a mouth on the statues was a black weal of shiny skin slit by six white holes. The bullet head had no visible ears and was set atop a massive torso. Arms and legs looked brutally powerful, and the "hands" that gripped the hatchway were covered with coarse hair. A flap at the base of its "chin" dropped and exposed sharp teeth.

If she'd never seen the shrine, it wouldn't have occurred to her that a creature that looked like this could be sentient; she would have simply thought it dangerous. Then she remembered locking the hatch when she went out. Without the security system on, it had bypassed the lock. Had it deliberately waited until the truck was empty? She stared up at this intruder, too frightened to think clearly or even to protest when it leaned forward, yanked the amplifier from her grasp, and clasped it to its chest in a manner that said, "Mine!" Its eyes never leaving hers, it stepped onto the ramp and started toward her.

She backed away, up against the truck, pulled the gun

from her pocket, and then hesitated. So small a weapon might only enrage an animal of this size. As she stood frozen with indecision, the horned turtle came running, as if still intent on entering the truck now that it saw a chance. Its locomotion at top speed gave the impression it was jumping over invisible hoops. It wheezed with each impact as it bounded up the ramp and slammed into the intruder's legs.

There was a blinding flash and the turtle went flying. A mass of ball lightning shot off across the pool and disappeared beneath the overhanging cliff. Creature and artifact were gone, vanished. The air smelled of ozone and singed hair.

Jenny was so frightened that she had to lean against the truck to stand. Several minutes passed before she recovered enough to move, and then she saw the turtle. It lay near Eli's truck. Wisps of smoke drifted up from the body.

She limped over. Light spots were still dancing in front of her eyes, but she could see enough. The turtle's legs were limp, its head and neck fully extended. Shell and horn were charred, and all its fur was singed to ash. It was dead.

"Poor turtle," she whispered, dropping on her knees. "Were you just curious—or did you deliberately save my life? Are you the lion after all?"

She took a deep breath to sigh, and the smell nearly gagged her. Moving like someone drugged, she unhooked the trowel from her belt and began to dig a hole.

When she reached over to slide the turtle into its grave, a tear plunked on the ruined shell. "I'm sorry," she apologized, and wiped the spot dry with her forefinger. The shell was still warm from the electrocution.

When the grave was mounded, she put a rock on top and sat beside it, exhausted and temporarily at a loss for what to do. The hatch to their truck was still open. Seeing it reminded her; she paged her father.

"Muffin!" His voice seemed strained through the tiny wrist-band speaker. "I was about to call you."

"Dad—"

"You've got to see this. Talk about glory holes—our friend Rothman barely skimmed the surface. I sincerely doubt he ever saw this particular place—"

"Dad—"

"There are old vaults here."

"Listen to me!" She almost shouted.

"Jenny? Are you in pain? You sound odd."

"We've got to get away from here! There was a thing— like the statues in the cave, only this one was alive. It got into the truck. When the turtle hit it, it changed into ball lightning, like I saw last night when I turned on the security system." She realized she wasn't making much sense.

He didn't answer for a few seconds, and then he asked, "Are you hurt?" The jubilation was gone from his voice. He sounded tired.

"No, but I'm scared."

"How did it get in the truck?"

"I was outside—but I'd locked it—"

"Did it damage anything?"

"I don't know." She hadn't thought of that.

"Are you in danger now?"

Before she could answer, she heard Eli in the background and then her father's voice, muffled as if he'd put his hand over his wrist. There was a pause and then Sadler said, "We'll be back as fast as we can."

She didn't see or hear an animal as she walked back to the truck. All the birds had disappeared or fallen silent. A few bugs went on about their business. But then, how sensitive are bugs? she thought. Clouds and fog were lowering over the valley. The air was full of cold mist.

She hesitated at the ramp, then entered, gun in hand. Nothing seemed disturbed. The hatch closed properly; the security system went on. Then she noticed two scorch marks on the instrument panel and began a systematic check.

Everything worked until she reached the flight system and the computer said, "I'm sorry. Lift and navigational systems are inoperative. Damage exceeds self-repair capacity. A technician is required, along with new circuitry chips." An on-screen schematic flashed in three separate places to illustrate the problem.

"Do you mean we're stuck here?" She sat down at the thought.

"A technician is required," the computer repeated in its calm voice. "I am programmed to contact the Service Center at Tanin Port. Do you authorize that procedure?"

"Yes!" said Jenny. "The sooner the better."

"Thank you." The computer went still, and a flashing yellow button indicated it was speaking with the Port Computer. Minutes passed while she sat and wondered if the damage had been deliberate, or the accidental result of that lightning flash—or whatever the creature had done. The systems damaged seemed too selective to be accidental—but why would the thing want to keep them here? To frighten them? To get all the amplifiers back?

"The Service Center has been contacted and understands the problem. A technician will arrive with new chips in approximately twenty-six hours," the computer announced. "Should you require assistance in the interim, Port Security asks that you advise them immediately." Her automatic, "Thank you," got an automatic, "You're welcome."

Half an hour passed before she saw the bikes approaching. She turned off the security system and went out to meet them. Once assured that she was physically unharmed, her father seemed to regard her story with less than total belief. He made her tell it twice, and then dug up the turtle to see for himself that it had been electrocuted.

"Very well," he said, shoving dirt over the remains with his boot. "I'll go check the truck." He ignored the fact that she'd already done that.

Jenny exchanged glances with Eli, then squatted down and reburied the turtle properly. "Why doesn't he want to believe me?" she asked as she dug.

"We found a glory hole. He doesn't want to leave."

"But we can't go until the truck is fixed."

"I could fly you out. I told him so. One at a time." He knelt down to help her build a rock cairn over the grave. "My truck's too small to take you both and the things we found. And he won't leave them."

"Why not?"

"People get like that with jewels. They don't think any more."

"You found jewels?"

"We'll be safe here until the truck's repaired." Sadler's return interrupted Jenny's question. "The security system still functions. There's no need for panic. As I keep telling you, we're seeing natural phenomena we don't understand. With all those metal trees, this spot may be a natural lightning rod . . . and we don't know what's buried beneath the surface. Their technology was quite advanced. . . ." His voice trailed off as he studied their immediate surroundings.

The fog was heavier now. The river had become a dark band at the bottom of a slope. Nothing could be seen beyond. To the west only the pool and enclosing cliff were visible.

"We came back just in time, Eli. Another hour and we'd have been lost out there in this."

"Aren't you at all frightened?" Jenny asked, exasperated. "Can't you admit that we might be in danger?"

He studied her face for a moment, then said, "Yes . . . I'm concerned. I wasn't counting on the truck's not starting. That limits our choices—should a *real* emergency arise."

A cloud shadow moved, and the glare of the mist softened, darkened. Thunder rumbled through the fog. Eli scanned the sky, his face troubled.

"Was that real thunder?" Jenny asked him, and when he didn't answer, said, "Why don't you leave while you can?"

"Because you can't," he said, "And I brought you here."

"It appears the area is to get much-needed rain." Sadler reached out and helped her to her feet. "We'd better put the bikes away and get indoors." Seeing her expression as she limped along, he gave her a mollifying smile. "Consider the facts, Jenny. Until we entered that cavern the only tracks in there were animals'. The place had been deserted for who knows how many centuries. And that big hunting animal—surely it wouldn't live there if the ants were real?"

"That thing I saw was real, and it was dangerous," she insisted.

But he only shook his head. "Real lightning, yes, but nothing more. It left no tracks, no trail. See for yourself."

"I saw," she said. "You didn't."

He shook his head and shrugged, not wanting to argue, and went to unload the collecting bags from the freight box on the nearest bike. She went into the truck and sat on her bed, feeling oddly helpless as she watched him bring in an armload of bags, set them on the floor, and then step aside while Eli brought in an even bigger load.

"It's starting to rain now. Listen." The boy gestured toward the pool. "The bell trees will ring."

"I'll turn on the recorder. Perhaps they ring some message, some ancient mathematical code." James Sadler grinned at them, concern apparently forgotten. "And while I'm at it, I'll turn on both cameras—the infrared may record some interesting things if we give it a chance. And—"

"Shhh," pleaded Eli, and the excited chatter ceased as Sadler settled himself at the control panel.

Raindrops made silent polka dots on the ramp. Then from the pool Jenny heard what sounded like an antique music box, playing at slow speed, but instead of being tinny, the notes were round as raindrops and totally pure.

After listening at the door, she put her raincape on and went out and sat beneath the truck to hear more clearly. A raindrop rang the first leaf it struck, rolled off and tapped the leaf below with a lighter touch, and waited to be joined by other drops until their accumulation ran and splashed new notes. There was no melody or pattern, not at first, but separate notes so distinct that after careful listening she could identify each tree's sound. The small leaves at the top were high notes; the broad leaves of the bottom branches hummed deep bass chords that blended with and blurred over the normal hiss of rain.

One tree sounded flat, off-key. On impulse she went over to investigate. It was the first tree they'd examined, the one from which they'd taken a core sample from the root, not knowing at the time that they were vandalizing a work of art. If damaging the root ruined the sound, were these trees an instrument that could somehow be keyed and controlled, the organ for this ruined cathedral? And if their designers wore those amplifiers and listened to these trees—did they experience religious ecstasy through sound? Or pay penance through the pain of hearing? Or were they merely deaf?

She walked beside the pool, listening, trying to understand, and it occurred to her that every rain, every wind gust, every temperature change would create variations in this music, endless variations on a single theme, like the statues, but infinite. Was that the purpose of them— like Buddhist prayer wheels turning in the wind, endlessly entreating heaven, praying effortless prayers for a race long dead? Or celebrating them?

Dimly, almost distantly, she heard her father calling, "Jenny, come in now," and was angered by his intrusion into her thoughts. She wanted to hear the music, to understand, to be free of what she was and would be, to be free of him. And then, remembering his image as it sat in that round room insisting that he wanted to "hear the music"—she turned and hurried back around the pool. Perhaps it wasn't wise to understand an alien mind.

Before she reached the truck, the gentle rain increased to a shower and the music of the bell trees altered from separate, haunting notes to intricate melody, to a rush of sound of frightening complexity. It wasn't that it was so loud, but that the tones were constant. There was no pause, no rest between one vibration's ending and the next's beginning. Her inner ears began to ache, and her chest felt odd. She clutched her hood around her face and limped faster.

"That's why I didn't come with you," Eli said as she closed the hatch behind her and leaned against it to catch her breath. He sat curled up on a seat across from her. "If it rains hard, you can't get too close to them."

"Why didn't you tell me?"

"Because you wanted to see how they worked, and that's the only way to do it. If you warn people of the bad part of things, you make them miss a lot of good. You would have missed seeing the leaves tremble as they sing, as if for that moment they were alive. And maybe they are."

She paused, cape half off, intrigued by the idea. "Have the trees grown taller since you were here last?"

"No. But neither have I."

"The computer can't make sense of the sounds. How about some lunch? It's late." Sadler got up from the control panel where he'd been fiddling with buttons. "You'll be staying, Eli," and without waiting for an answer, he turned on the security system. The truck, soundproofed for high-speed flight, closed out most of the bells.

It was amazing, Jenny thought with gratitude, how food could cheer you. Even freeze-dried food. A bowl of tomato soup, a proto-burger with brown mustard, and she felt much better. Even the fact that the fog outside was now so thick they could barely see the trees didn't seem to matter. They were inside, warm and dry, with the security system turned on. They might be safe until help came.

EIGHTEEN

BACK ON HER BED, BOOTS OFF, FEET ELEVATED, SHE looked through the collecting bags and better understood her father's reluctance to leave. He'd found what they'd come to Tanin for. Rothman hadn't exaggerated; there were gems packed in small cases, burnished metal boxes holding jewels more brilliant than diamond fancies, faceted to refract the slightest ray of light. When the lid of each case opened, the gems inside blazed so that she breathed, "Ahh!" as if she'd seen a burst of fireworks.

"The place we found them, Muffin," Sadler said enthusiastically, reliving the moment with all the detail of mankind's ancient delight in hunting stories, "the place suggests the ruins of subbasements when a building's razed—in this case centuries ago. The site's overgrown with trees. Animals kept staring at us, wondering what we wanted. I had just leaned against a flat stone when it caved in. When the dust settled, we saw this high narrow file room lined with shelves like wine racks. Half the compartments held scrolls, similar to the one Eli found, which I now own, and the rest held these jewel boxes—"

She interrupted him. "Where are the scrolls?"

"We didn't have time to gather much. You called. But we'll go back tomorrow. You can come along if you're up to it."

"Is it safe to leave the truck alone?"

"Oh, yes . . ." he said vaguely, and she realized he'd already forgotten. "Well . . . we'll work something out."

And he went on with his story. "Eli will get half, of course, but even so . . ."

Eli sat on the floor, a box of gems open in front of him, a jeweler's loupe in his left eye. One by one, he was inspecting the lot, as absorbed as if he were totally alone. She watched him as she listened to her father. The boy didn't look up.

The fog lifted, but clouds kept the valley dark as twilight. The bell trees rang. Rain poured off the roof, the channel strips overflowing. Rivulets down the windows blurred what little view remained. Her father's softly cadenced speech combined with other sounds. She yawned, mouth closed to avoid being rude; her eyelids dropped. Her father went on talking, high on hidden treasures.

"Jenny!" Eli's urgent whisper woke her. He was standing in the hatchway looking out into the night. The rain had stopped. "Jenny!" Then, glancing over at her, he said, "Dr. Sadler's gone outside. I can't see him anywhere."

She got up as quickly as she could and joined him at the door. The air smelled cold and sweet, as it had on the mountaintop. No stars shone.

"Why did he go out?" She whispered because he was whispering.

Eli shook his head. "He was sitting in the pilot's seat, half asleep, and all of a sudden he got up, put on his boots, turned off the security system, and went out. I asked him where he was going, but he didn't say."

"Dad?" Jenny called into the darkness. "Dad? Are you out there?" and waited for an answer. None came. "I'm going to turn the security system back on," she threatened. Still no answer. "Did you hear me?"

As she moved to the control panel, she noticed the vu-screens. Both cameras were still on. One screen was dark, but the infrared picture was computer enhanced. In that camera's view the pool and walkway were cold blue, the bell trees glowed yellow as if they were hot. In the right-hand corner of the screen she recognized the pale green figure of James Sadler, walking toward the cliff. Beneath the overhang moved a procession of pale figures, creatures from the cave.

"Eli!" She grabbed his arm and pointed to the screen. "Call him! Yell! As loud as you can!"

Both of them called again and again, until their shouts echoed back from the cliffs, but he gave no indication of hearing. As they watched, Sadler began to run. Before he reached the pale figures they stopped and turned his way— almost, Jenny thought, as if they'd been waiting for him.

"He's going with ghosts," Eli said in tones of disbelief. "Why would he do that?"

"To find out what they really are." There was a hint of exasperation in Jenny's voice. "He doesn't believe in ghosts." She went and got an ace bandage from the first-aid drawer and sat down with her boots. "I'm going after him. He shouldn't go alone." At Eli's deep sigh she looked up from wrapping her ankle. "You don't have to go along. I know it's against your rules."

"Are you sure?" he said. Distractedly he pulled his hood up over his head and then pulled it down again. "That's the trouble with getting involved with people—I get blurred around the edges until I don't know what I think or where I stop and they begin. And then they go away, as if it never happened."

There was a lost bewilderment in his eyes for that moment that made Jenny forget everything else and simply want to hug him. But then he said, "I'll get the bikes out. You shouldn't go there alone."

Before they left, she turned on the outside lights and took the portable control so she could reactivate the security system once they were clear of its range. They didn't need more unexpected visitors in the truck.

The night was cold and so dark the headlights on the bikes seemed faint. She shivered in the breeze of riding and wished she'd thought to wear her sweater underneath her jacket. Why had her father been fool enough to go off into the night alone? That made her angry—such willful inconsiderateness. Of course, if he'd come to Tanin alone, she wouldn't have known anything about this. Maybe he took chances like this whenever he went off by himself and no one ever knew about it. But why would he do that?

They rode the walkway by the bell trees. Puddles flew and hissed as the fat tires rolled through them. Now and then a drop of water falling from one leaf to another produced a sudden musical *ploink*, but those were the only sounds. Jenny had the strangest feeling that she and Eli were the only living things in this whole world. It was all she could do to keep from making a U-turn and racing back to the truck, getting into bed, and hiding under the covers.

Halfway there, Eli signaled for a stop, and she pulled up beside him. Instead of talking, he pointed. The pool was sparkling with blue ripples. There were lights up inside the cavern. "Do you want to go on?" he whispered.

"Maybe Dad took a torch with him."

"His torch wouldn't be blue."

As he said that, she thought of the ball lightning and the turtle and pictured her father, lying on the ground, smoke coming up from his clothes. How would she tell her mother?

"You want to wait here and I'll go look?" Eli's gallant whisper broke through her morbid imaginings.

"No! I'll go. You wait," she said, and pulled away. She saw the beam of his headlight recede and then almost catch up with her. He was following.

It seemed to take forever to circle that last half mile around the end of the pool and up the ramp. She wasn't even worried about the chance of meeting the giant guinea pig again. Compared to what she'd been through since, that animal was nothing—well, almost nothing. She made a hard right turn, rolled to a halt on the floor of the cavern, and shut off the bike's power. Eli pulled up beside her, and both sat and stared.

The light was coming from the statues. All their eyes shone blue. Row on row, tier atop tier, high up into the domed ceiling, curving back into the darkness, endless, countless statues, all with sapphire eyes aglow.

"Look at them." Eli's awestruck whisper echoed Jenny's thoughts. "I didn't see them all before . . . so many . . ."

What kind of minds would do this, she wondered, build endless hollow images and hide them in a cave? What sort of madness was this?

"Look!" Eli whispered. "There, in the center."

She saw a moving shadow, elongated by back lighting, then a figure darker than the shadow. It was her father, his wine-red pants and jacket turned black by the blue light, his face reflecting a shade of bluish-pink. He was strolling along with his hands clasped behind his back, casually surveying the scene.

Her impulse was to call him—he was less than thirty yards away—but she hesitated. Something else might answer. She glanced at Eli and shivered; his face was a ghastly gray in this blue light, his lips deep purple. She

/150

wondered if she looked as revolting, and decided she must. "You stay here. I'm going to ride over and get him," she whispered.

"I wouldn't do that—" Eli's whisper was drowned out by a roar of sound, gibberish through an amplifier. Both jumped and Jenny saw her father turn and come to attention. His arms went rigid at his sides, and he raised his face to the blue-eyed images. There was a second blare of sound, then speech.

Jenny felt sick to her stomach. That was her father's voice, speaking as he had before, as the image in the center of rings. If she rode over to him now, would he glitch and disappear? She shifted on her seat, ready to start the bike, but Eli touched her arm and shook his head.

"In the manner of your Kind you violate our sacred place." James Sadler accused himself with no feeling. "Your first act upon arrival was to wantonly destroy harmonics older than your species." With a yelp of protest he twisted away from the spot where he stood, flailing the air as if freeing himself from ropes. "I will not be manipulated to parrot your thoughts!" he shouted, his voice his own again. "Who are you? What are you? If we can communicate, why can't we be civilized about it? This shrine has been deserted for centuries. Why are you here now? Why—"

He jerked as if he'd received an electric shock, and went rigid again. There was a pause, and he resumed the computer-like tone, but more slowly. "We chose this world long before your species came to scavenge. Here we sought and gained our grasp of holy order.

"Understanding simplicity would reveal the unifying link with all matter, all energy. Our artisans practiced discipline. Crystals were cut—matter and light, sagas woven— particles of imagination. Enhancers of all sounds were created by the—" The word was garbled and sounded like "klikthors." "This holy place was built, each shaping in his own image the memory of his need for pure form."

Sadler stopped talking, but remained at rigid attention.

"Are they saying they can change from matter to energy?" she whispered to Eli. "Is that what they mean by pure form?"

"Shhh," Eli cautioned. "If they can control Dr. Sadler's mind, they can control ours. They may hear our thoughts."

That idea silenced her until it occurred to her that if they *could* read minds, it didn't matter if she talked or not. If they were all the things they said they were, why did they need a ship? And all these stage sets and props—like idols with shining eyes, and mechanical ants?

"Some lost faith. Failed to attain conversion. They fled the clusters for the chaos of the wild beyond the barrier. They took kwikthors with them, to insure privacy and discipline until meditation brought release. The living chaos killed them. . . . They were fragmented by listening, distracted by incidentals. But we watch over them. We are the stewards."

Sadler had been reactivated so abruptly that the words rushed out at twice his usual speed. If they can make him talk that fast, Jenny thought worriedly, can they speed up or slow down the rest of him, turn him into a human version of one of their ants? Remembering his exhaustion of the day before, she turned her bike on again and eased it into gear.

"What are you going to do?" Eli whispered.

"Go and get him." As she spoke, she saw something move beside one of the statues; light was reflecting off a pale blue halo.

"If they control his mind, he can't come with you," Eli said. "He might not even know we're there."

Jenny felt a wave of tiredness settle over her and knew that if she sat here much longer trying to weigh unknown dangers, she'd end up doing nothing at all. Sometimes one had to take chances.

"Look at the center arch, the left-hand side. What do you see?"

"Something's there . . ." he said slowly, "like a shadow—wearing an amplifier. They can hear us!"

She ignored that. "When I say go, you ride over and get Dad, and I'll go distract their attention. Leave your lights off."

"What if they turn into lightning?"

"They can't do two things at once."

"How do you know?"

"Because they let us sit here all this time."

Eli looked as if he didn't think that was much of an argument, and she knew it wasn't. But she didn't have time to discuss it. "Yes or no?" she whispered.

"Yes."

Without waiting to hear more, she released the brake and sped away. When still some distance from the center arch, she turned on the headlight, bright, and screamed— short piercing screams of the type and pitch that hurt ears without amplifiers. The screams echoed and re-echoed.

In the light beam she saw two of the halo-wearing aliens clamp their furry hands against the back of their heads and writhe in pain. From behind the pedestal came muffled thumping sounds as if some animal were trapped inside the hollow statue, trying to batter its way out.

"Jenny? Is that you? My God!—Eli?"

He was free! His voice was normal. She aimed at the arch as if she were going to ride right in, and at the last possible moment she swerved away. Halfway through the turn, the bike teetered, unstable at high speed. Only a quick balancing act saved her from tipping over. Settling back onto the seat, she saw two things: Eli's taillight as he stopped to pick up her father, and one of the ants approaching from the left. It was fear of having the ant grab her from behind that made her circle back toward it. The ant reared, antennae waving.

NINETEEN

ALTHOUGH THE NIGHT WAS LESS THAN HALF OVER, THE
ghema was headed for home. She'd had no luck hunting.
The animals were restless and ran before she could get
near. After ranging many miles without food, she was tired
and in a filthy temper. She paused for a drink at the river,
then waded in and swam across, shook the muddy water
from her fur, and padded on.

At the top of the slope she detoured around the two
unknowns near the pool. The larger form emitted light.
Both smelled wrong. A ground draft carried the scent of
burned animal soaked by loose wet soil. She paused to
sniff more thoroughly, then growled, ill at ease. Her den
was safe and warm and dry. She broke into a loping run.

The lights glinting off the pool were no different to her
than blue moonlight and were ignored, but the scent of
interlopers on the ramp raised her ire. *She* was the dom-
inant animal here. She had fled them once, but not again.
To allow them dominance meant giving up her den, her
hunting grounds, forcing her to fight another ghema for
its territory. She knew instinctively she was too old for
that.

With a yowl of rage she bounded up the ramp and
charged across the floor, head down, aiming to ram the
first interloper she saw and tear it to bits. A beam of
blinding light swept over her right eye, causing her to
veer.

Jenny saw the animal only as it rushed past and slammed

into the ant. Her bike speed carried her beyond the line of view, but she heard a crash against one of the pedestals, followed by a second impact. Stone fell from somewhere and shattered on the floor. The animal began to scream, almost human screams of pain—if a human weighed twelve hundred pounds and had a head large enough to produce such resonance. The sound was so huge, so shocking, in this natural echo chamber, that she automatically braked to a stop and turned to see what was happening. More stones fell. There was a grating sound. From the farther recesses of the cavern came a rumbling crash, as if a wall had collapsed. Dust thickened the light beam.

The blue lights were going out, image by image, row on row. As the screams continued, whole sections of the cavern went dark. Ball lightning glowed out of the upper arches and came floating, tumbling, rolling downward beneath the roof to slip out under the overhang. The screaming went on and on.

She turned her bike until the headlight focused on the giant guinea pig. It stood diminished, head down, shuddering against the pedestal of the center arch. On the floor beside it lay the bodies, minus the heads, of two ants. Legs had been broken off and scattered. Half the body spines were missing.

And then she saw the cause of the animal's agony; spines protruded from its eyes and muzzle. With spine-filled paws it was clawing at its face, and in trying to end its pain was increasing it.

She reached into her muff pocket and found the handgun still there. If she aimed between the eyes? Her hands were shaking so she had to rest the gun atop the handlebars. It took six shots before the screaming stopped, four more before the animal sank to its knees and toppled over. The body convulsed, then went limp.

A second headlight beam crossed hers. The other bike pulled up beside her. "Are you all right?" The question seemed to come from a long way off. She felt her father's hand on her shoulder as he gave her a gentle shake. "Are you in shock? Can you ride? We have to get out of here— the place is collapsing."

She saw the second tier of statues trembling nervously. "Yes, of course," she said. "You lead the way." Their beams swept over the idol smiling its forever smile. In front of it lay the ghema and the ants, like offerings. On the floor beside it were small piles of blue sand.

The bikes were almost down the ramp when the full collapse began. Dust rained down over them. The ground shook beneath their wheels. Stone fragments tumbled or flew into the dark water, causing alarming splashes. The pool slopped and surged.

It was strange what the mind could do, Jenny thought as they rode back to the trucks. So long as it could make the muscles obey, one cold level of the mind could keep you going, get you away from anything, and ignore all the other visions in your brain. It could let you ride a bike, steer around a boulder, feel the mist on your face, the throb in your right foot, see blue lightning in the clouds above the desert, be aware that someone was talking, re- member and imagine the pain of a wounded animal, and killing it. There was a separate self somewhere inside the brain, hidden, like an invisible rock over which the stream flowed. And the stream was almost incidental; it was the rock that counted, the Self no one ever saw.

"Whatever they are, they did learn something extraor- dinary here," Sadler was saying. "They sound like physicists turned high priests—or turned mad with knowledge. And yet they appear to have rejected that knowledge—or gone beyond it. I taped it all, you know—I wish I'd thought to take a camera. I'm still not sure if what we saw were real life forms." He talked on and on.

Neither Eli nor Jenny said a word the whole way back. She turned off the security system as they approached the truck.

"Why do I get the impression your joint silence is based more on disapproval than fear or fatigue?" the man asked as they pulled up beside the bike bay and dismounted.

"Because mine is. You shouldn't go off like that when you have responsibilities—" Jenny stopped, not wanting to embarrass Eli by creating a scene.

"Responsibilities." Jim Sadler repeated the word as if it depressed him. "You're right, of course. I have responsibilities." His voice lightened and became almost pleading. "But there are times, Jenny, when you want to do things *now*, without thought, because if you stop to think, the chance is gone and never comes again. You didn't stop to think the first time you ran up that ramp alone—and that's how tonight really began."

He helped Eli push the bikes in and closed the freight hatch, while Jenny numbly wondered if discovering the cave made tonight her fault. Perhaps so—in her father's mind.

"Good night," Eli said abruptly, and headed toward his truck.

"Aren't you staying with us?" Sadler called after him.

"No. It will be too crowded."

"But you stayed with us last night."

"Yes." The warped hatch on the little truck sang open, then shut.

"Apparently he, too, is on the side of responsibility."
Sadler gave her a rueful smile. "Perhaps because he has
none. You can't understand now, but you will, with time,
when you're my age. It's all a matter of perspective."

After she'd gone to bed, she lay looking out at Eli's light
shining in the dark and wondered if he was sleeping with
the lights on. Or maybe he was cold, too, and just couldn't
get warm. Her father lay stretched out on his bed, far too
quiet to be sleeping.

She tensed with every move he made, as if he were a
stranger. She had always viewed him as a set piece, a benign image called "Dad," but being *Dad* was, she was
learning, only one aspect of his life, and not the primary
one. He, too, must have a Self no one ever saw, a Self
that was untouchable. Yet if she let this barrier grow, she'd
never reach across it.

"Dad?" She whispered although she knew he was awake.
"Yes?"

"Do you get tired of being what you are?"

There was a long silence before he said, "Often. Do
you?"

"Yes. Does it get worse as you get older?"

Again there was a thoughtful silence. "No. It gets easier. You learn to accept limitations, to be what others expect. But every so often you must break away and run, as
I do on these trips, to someplace where you can be yourself—if you can remember what that is."

"Does it have to be dangerous?" she asked, and heard
him chuckle.

"No, but that helps. That way you appreciate home more
when you get back."

She considered that. "Is that why you went after them
tonight? For the thrill of it?"

"Partly. But I wanted to know what they are. The best of crops won't sell land on a haunted world. I'll have to have a study done, have researchers stay out here in isolated places, interview the miners." He talked on, slipping away into the role of businessman worrying about an investment, avoiding the true issue.

"Dad," she interrupted, "that doesn't excuse your thoughtlessness, or exposing us all to danger. I could picture you being killed and me worrying how I'd tell Mother. How do you think that made me feel? That's why I followed you."

"It didn't occur to me you would. You were asleep—I'm sorry. But also very glad you did. Now we'd better get some rest. Would you like a sleeping tablet? I'm going to have one. I don't want to dream."

When his light went off again, she listened to his breathing deepen into sleep and wondered what he would have been if he hadn't been James Sadler. She'd have to ask him sometime—when there was more space between them. Her mother was wrong; some people shouldn't be seen outside their roles.

A raindrop struck the window. The leaf of a bell tree rang, then another and another, each whole and separate tones.

They woke to find sunshine and the animals had returned, but Eli and his truck were gone. He'd left a note on their ramp, weighed down by a rock. "The magic's gone," was all it said. "I think that means he believes we'll be safe here now." Sadler handed the note to Jenny, who read it and felt her eyes fill. She blinked and said nothing.

For the rest of her life, when she thought of Tanin, she remembered that morning ride out to the cliffs to bring back the rest of the treasure. The room was gone, buried beneath tons of stone, as if subsurface chambers had collapsed and brought part of the cliff tumbling down. One battered tree, incongruously green, stuck up out of the rubble. She remembered that tree, and images of blue sky and fluffy clouds, wildlife, rimrock, and hoodoos of beige and pink and white. The bell trees and the cavern became separate things, buried deeper in her mind, surreal images that sometimes drifted into dreams of childhood.

TWENTY

JENNY DIDN'T REALIZE THE FULL EFFECT OF BEING frightened for so many days until she saw the port come into view and thought it was the most wonderful place she'd ever seen. The sea, the beach, the airport, every shabby building pleased her. And there were people, dear people. Even the Institute looked cozy sprawled atop its hill, enclosed by its chain-link fencing, secure from danger. When she stepped out of the airtruck, only an innate sense of dignity kept her from kissing the ground.

No one seemed surprised to see them back a week early. The truck's breakdown and her injury were more than adequate reasons. And when she told the people at the medical center that she had been attacked by "a giant guinea pig," her description of the creature became part of local folklore. In years past miners had been killed by animals like that. That she survived to tell the tale made her unique.

The first two days back she did little more than sleep and eat and sleep again while her bruises changed muddy colors and her ankle sank back to normal size. She saw her father only at mealtimes, where there was little chance to talk privately. He spent those days and part of each evening working in the truck, "Packing film and fragile artifacts for shipment," he told Drs. Bower and Rule. Jenny thought, correctly, that what he was really doing was secreting the gems somewhere in their luggage where they wouldn't excite the curiosity of local customs people.

"I've tried to locate Eli," he told her the second evening when he stopped by her room to say good night. "Port Security says he's returned, but they don't know where he is. We have to find out what he wants done with his share of our treasure. I'd like to market it on Earth— we'll get twice as much as he would from local dealers, without revealing the source. But either way, he'll be quite rich."

"Is he all right? Did Security know?"

"I'm sure he is. He's very self-sufficient." He turned to leave. "If we don't hear from him in a couple of days, I'll make arrangements at the local bank. Oh, by the way, half our share is yours, of course." He smiled as he thought of something else. "I'll bet you never imagined, when you read Rothman's journal, how profitably your time was spent."

Eli probably doesn't want to see us again, she thought after her father had gone. I made him break all his rules, do stupid, dangerous things he'd never do alone. He'll probably never be anybody's guide again.

She got out of bed and went over to the window, where her collection of seashells and beach pebbles lay spread across the sill, picked up a small tube of bubble-wrap, and took it back to bed to open. Light flashed from the long, flawless topaz crystal from the cave at Wok Lake. Looking at it, she saw Eli as he gave it to her, saw his face as she patched him up in the cave, saw him walk away. She didn't want to go without telling him good-bye.

She had five days before the shuttle came. She spent them exploring with one of the bikes. Equipped with an aerial map from Port Security, and with lunch and water packed in the carrier, she would leave early in the morning and not come back until dusk.

By studying the map and by remembering which way he walked over the hills, she found what she thought was his house. It was less than two miles from the Institute, hidden down a tunnel-like lane that led to a bare spot that was both landing pad and turnaround. Beyond, trees sheltered a building made of adobe blocks. Both shutters and door were closed. She called hello but no one answered.

Leaving the bike beside a shed in which a rusty land car sat on blocks, waiting for front wheels, she walked up to the house. There was a water tank and pump along the south wall and other equipment she couldn't identify. The whole place wasn't much bigger than her bedroom at home.

She walked around the little building, trying to imagine what it was like to live out here alone. What did he do when it rained at night, or a storm blew in from the sea? Off in the trees a bird sang of green leaves, dappled shadows, and peace.

From the front of the house the ocean beckoned a mile beyond. The trees ended in a rock outcropping with roots gnarling over the stone. On the rocks sat several animals and a dumpy bronze-feathered bird. All fled when she got too close.

In the hollows of the rocks were hidden pans of seed and water. She puzzled over that until she decided this must be Eli's way of keeping pets. They could enjoy the food; he could enjoy their company; they could see each other clearly and never have to touch.

Back at the house, she tried the door, and to her surprise it opened. Sunshine lit a quiet room. The walls were white; the rug was blue carpeting salvaged from a shuttle. The company logo was still visible. There was a fireplace, two salvaged pilot's chairs on wooden frames, a narrow bed with white blankets, and books—all sorts of books. A workbench filled one wall, with tools above it, neatly racked. In wall niches beautiful crystal formations glowed from hidden lights. Two doors led off the main room. Both were closed.

There were no pictures, nothing posted to proclaim taste or personality, and yet the room looked like him. Each item in it stood alone, distinct, and gained from its aloofness.

As she closed the door and walked back to her bike, she felt a sense of loss, almost sure they'd never meet again. She went back to the house each day, but he was never home.

Each evening she would sit on Eli's bench and watch the sunset. The sky here had so many stars, and unlike Earth's, erased or dimmed by lights, these looked new and clean. It occurred to her as she sat there one evening, content to be alone, that if she stayed in a place like this too long, she wouldn't like Earth much when she got back. It would seem too crowded, too complex, too busy, and she wondered if that, not the lure of treasure, was what kept the miners here.

The days she counted as "leftovers" passed. The shuttle came in, and they would leave with it in the morning. The airtruck had been stripped of all their personal things. The baggage was packed and all but hand luggage had been sent to the spaceport to be weighed and loaded.

The last night there she couldn't sleep, and sometime after midnight she dressed and went out for a walk. Pole lights lit the main drive. In their small worlds of light insects circled madly. The air smelled clean and faintly of the sea. She walked the garden paths and then followed the drive up through the orchard. The trees whispered with furtive rustlings and squeakings—fruit cats prowling for dinner.

From habit, she followed the drive to the gate. She had ridden through it so often lately that she could see the path the bike wheels left in the grass. She opened the gate and went on.

The familiar hills were strange in the dark. The grass was wet with dew. Sounds she hadn't given a second thought to inside the fence made her heart beat faster out here. She tried to concentrate on admiring a moon rising out of the sea, but that didn't help much. She would go as far as Eli's bench, she decided, and then she could turn back, proving to herself that she really wasn't afraid of the dark. She ran the last fifty yards and sat down on the still sun-warm bench with a sense of reaching a haven.

"Don't be scared. It's me."

She jumped before her mind said *Eli,* and she saw him, a gray shadow blending with the night on the other end of the bench.

"It's a nice night for a walk," she said when she regained her breath.

"Yes."

"I've been hunting you."

"Yes, I saw you."

"Why didn't you—" Suddenly she was embarrassed. "Would you like me to leave?"

"No."

There was an awkward silence.

"The treasure room caved in. Did you see that?"

"Yes."

"My father says you're going to be very rich when he sells the jewels on Earth. He's left instructions for you at the bank. You'll have to talk to them."

"That's nice. I think I'll like that."

She smiled, thinking most people would have screamed for joy, especially if they were as poor as Eli seemed to be, and yet he called wealth "nice" and thought no more about it.

There was another silence. "Did your stitches come out nicely?"

"Yes. Not like your orange." He hesitated and then said, "Your leg's O.K. I saw you running."

"Why did you leave us without saying good-bye?"

His heel scuffed against the stone as he tucked one leg beneath him and shifted to face her. "I didn't want to see your father again—because I don't like him. And I didn't want to say good-bye to you, because I do. Saying good-bye isn't bad if you're going to see people again, but if you're not, good-byes end things."

"Oh." She thought that over until she understood. "You're not coming to Earth?"

"I don't think so."

"Not ever?"

"Not for a long time."

"Why not?"

"I couldn't stand it there," he said simply.

"But it's nice—or it can be," she protested. "You can live with us. You'll be rich enough to do anything. And you're my friend, and I'll see to it—"

"Jenny," he interrupted gently. "You like me here. But would you there? You're away from what you usually are. You're lonesome." She was going to talk, and he raised his hand. "Picture me in your world. Would I belong?"

"No . . . probably not," she admitted. "Not until you got used to it . . . if you did. But I'd still like you. And so would my friends. And my mother would like you a lot. Couldn't you stand being unhappy for a while? Long enough to get an education? To see if you liked it? You could always come back here." She thought of something else. "I'm going away to college. You could come with me. We'd both be strangers there."

"I don't know."

They were quiet for minutes, lost in their own thoughts. Below, along the beach, the waves drew scalloped white lines in the dark. An occasional bird cry could be heard above the noise of breakers walloping the offshore rocks.

"Eli?"

"Yes?"

"I have to go now."

"Oh."

"I'll miss you." She managed to say it clearly, without letting him know she was close to crying.

"Yes," he agreed, and she nearly laughed. A second later she was glad she hadn't. "I'll miss you, too," he said. "I'm sorry about that. I missed you all this week. I don't know why. It spoils things, you know, missing people."

"Isn't it better than not missing someone?"

"I don't know. I've never had anyone to miss before. I thought it would quit if I stayed by myself. But it didn't. Do you think it will?"

"I don't know."

"If it doesn't—and I never see you again . . . I'll walk you back."

The last she saw of Eli he stood outside the chain-link gate, one arm raised in a silent good-bye, and then he turned and ran. She was halfway down the drive when something made her stop and listen. From somewhere on the moonlit hill came a joyous whistle. She ran back to the gate.

"Jenny?" His voice came out of the starry night.

"Yes?"

"When I get there, will you come and meet me?"

"Yes!"

"Jenny—where do you live?"

ABOUT THE AUTHOR

H. M. Hoover is one of America's leading writers of science fiction for young people. She is the author of *The Delikon, The Rains of Eridan, The Lost Star, Return to Earth,* and *This Time of Darkness,* all published by Viking. Her latest book, *Another Heaven, Another Earth,* is an ALA Best Book.

Ms. Hoover lives near Washington, D. C., where she pursues her interests in natural history, archaeology, and history, as well as writing.